CATWOMEN FROM HELL

CATWOMEN FROM HELL

Contemporary short stories by women from Wales

Edited by

JANET THOMAS

HONNO MODERN FICTION

Published by Honno
'Ailsa Craig', Heol y Cawl, Dinas Powys,
South Glamorgan, Wales, CF6 4AH.

British Library Cataloguing in Publication Data

Catwomen From Hell
1. Title

ISBN 1 870206 40 1

Published with the financial support of the
Arts Council of Wales

Acknowledgements:
'Snakeskin Becomes Her' and 'Voodoo Cantata'
have been broadcast on BBC Radio 4;
'The Blackberry Season' was first published in *Corridor:*
Cambridge Feminist Review 1991; 'Ordinary Alice' was first
published in *The Big Issue* (April 6-12 1998).

Cover Image: 'Valley Girls II' by Christine Kinsey
Cover design by Chris Lee Design

Typeset and printed in Wales by Gwasg Dinefwr, Llandybïe

CONTENTS

FOREWORD

This is Honno's third contemporary short story anthology, aiming to give Welsh women the opportunity to see their work in print and to showcase the range, depth and imagination of current Welsh writing.

This time the stories were collected under the theme 'Wicked Women of Wales'. This was to give new and established writers the encouragement to be subversive, to tackle dark, dangerous subjects, to break away from the constraints of naturalism or simply to have fun.

But what is 'wicked'? Some stories see it simply as women who go against society's expectations of them, as in Siân James's moving 'Guilty' or Kitty Sewell's hilarious bikers gang 'CatWomen from Hell'. Indeed, it says something disturbing about women's continuing perception of their lives that very often the 'wicked' women are only doing what they want to do.

Some stories reclaim and reinvent traditional images of evil women from fairy tale and legend, as in Fiona Owen's haunting version of the wicked stepmother in 'Fish'. Many use the poetic possibilities of magic and superstition to play with the reader's expectations. Revenge has an ambiguous attraction in several stories and in others the women are cruel or cowardly, the authors brave enough to leave us sad and unsettled.

Overall – frightening and funny, sad and empowering – they are about taking or losing control. People at a moment of change. People on the edge. When I think of the collection as a whole, I visualise the heroine of Christine Harrison's 'The Palace of Anxieties', standing on the cliff, but with the feeling of wings on her back.

There is also a powerful sense of place in these stories.

All Wales is here – the city, mining valley, gossipy village, the sea and the mountainous countryside. Many stories are set outside Wales and it is vital that Welsh women living elsewhere do not feel alone. With some publishers still subscribing to the self-fulfilling prophecy that people are not interested in stories from Wales, Honno is playing its part in establishing a community of Welsh writers, visible, active and supporting each other. The collection also gives new writers the chance to feel part of that writing community. I am pleased that Lindsay Ashford and Chloë Heuch are seeing their work in print for the first time, and I hope others reading this will feel inspired to submit their work in the future.

My thanks to everyone who submitted stories, to Patricia Duncker for her support, and especially to Gwenllïan Dafydd and Eurwen Booth at Honno for this chance to work with them and for their endless encouragement. It was painful to choose from the over a hundred stories received. In the end I chose the ones that stayed with me, the ones that would not be left out. I hope you will find much to enjoy and move you here and maybe one or two that will leave you with the sense described in Tessa Hadley's wonderful 'Phosphorescence', 'of the great dazzle that was clinging to him, dripping off him, flashing round in his veins.'

Janet Thomas

PHOSPHORESCENCE

~

Tessa Hadley

The Cooley boys used to spend all their summers at their cottage in West Wales. They had a boat, so most of the time they were on the water, or playing cricket on the beach, or helping their mother who was restoring the cottage. For whole days that summer when Graham was thirteen she was up on the roof in shorts and T-shirt and old daps, reslating. Their father went off every day alone, to paint landscapes.

That summer as usual various friends and family came and went, either staying at the cottage or in the tiny primitive chalet at the other end of the meadow which Graham's mother had done up for overspill visitors. It was to the chalet that Claudia and her family came: the Cooleys didn't know them well, her husband was some sort of technician in Graham's father's lab at the university. Their children were too small to join in the Cooley boys' games.

At first Graham took no more notice of Claudia than of any of the others who swam in and out of focus on the far off adult surface of his world. Then she started to pay him attention in an extraordinary way. Fourth of five brothers, he was usually surprised enough if any of his parents' friends even remembered what school he was at and how old he was. Claudia, this grown-up mother of three children, began to make a point of sitting next to him. When they all squeezed into the back of the old Bedford van, or around the cottage table for lunch, or in the sitting room in the evening for cards and Monopoly, she simply sat up against him and then let the weight of her leg lie against his. They had bare legs, usually; he was still young enough for shorts even on cool days, and it was at the time when women wore short skirts. She shaved her legs, brown legs (his mother didn't): he saw the stubble, felt it. Sometimes, after a while, almost imperceptibly, she began to press, just slightly press. It always could just have been accidentally.

Probably she was doing it for a long time before he even noticed: he was thirteen, after all, sex had hardly occurred to him, not as a physical reality he could have in connection with other people. And even once he'd noticed, once he'd started to excitedly, scaredly, wait for her to choose her place, even then he couldn't be sure, not at first, that he wasn't just crazily making it all up.

And at this point he began to take notice of Claudia all the time, to hardly take notice of anything else. She was plump and blonde, pretty, untidy: he noticed that a button kept slipping undone on a blouse too tight across her bust, and that her clothes bought to be glamorous were crumpled because her children were endlessly clambering over her. Struggling down to the beach with a toddler on one arm and beach bags slung across her shoulder, she kept turning over on a sandal with a leather thong between her toes, and he heard her swear – *shit!* – in an undertone. And once he heard her snap at her husband, when she was trying to read the paperback book she brought down every day to the beach and the children interrupted her one after another to pee or for food or quarrels:- *If I don't get to finish this* bloody *sentence I'll scream!* Graham's parents never swore, he only knew those words from school and from his brothers.

Claudia was a perfectly competent adult. She brought down to the beach everything her family needed: costumes and towels and picnic and suntan oil and changing stuff for

2

the baby and racquets and balls. She fed them and soothed them all. One of her little girls stepped on a jellyfish and howled for half an hour before she fell asleep on Claudia's lap, while Claudia sat stroking her sticky salty hair. But when Graham watched her playing badminton with his brothers – dazzling against the sea, grunting and racing and scooping up the shuttlecock in halter top and John Lennon peaked cap – he saw that she was still young, not his kind of young, but Tim's and Alex's. That must be why she was still crazy enough to be doing this thing to him. She couldn't have done it to Tim or Alex because with them it would have been real, she would have had to acknowledge what was going on, they would have known. With him it was so completely, completely outside possibility. It couldn't be happening.

On the beach it wasn't possible to be squeezed side by side. But she found other ways: he'd feel a gritty sandpapery toe just making contact, or when she reached across him to hand out sandwiches, he'd get a scorch of the flesh of her arm against his shoulder. It was so subtle that no one, however scrupulously they watched, could ever have seen: it was a chain of innocent accidents only connected through his burning consciousness of her touch.

On the surface she was particularly nice to him, asking him about school, asking his opinions on things the others talked about, the boat, the weather. She chose him to explain to her the rules of Racing Demon, he had to play through the first couple of hands with her. When she leaned excitedly forward over the table to see what had been played – she was short-sighted but wouldn't wear her glasses – she wedged him heavily into the corner, he smelled her sweat. His mother complimented Claudia on how she drew Graham out: he was supposed to be the shy one in the family arrangement, Alex was the brainy one, Phil the sporty one, and so on.

He began to be hardly able to look at his mother. She was like a humming black space where something familiar and unquestioned had previously been: he couldn't hold her and Claudia in his mind at the same time. Passionately he began to love all the things Claudia did differently to his mother: she yawned when his mother waxed indignant about conservation or bureaucracy, she opened tins for her family's supper (the chalet kitchen was primitive: but his mother would have done a slow-cooking casserole), she flirted with his father, leaning over him to see how the day's painting had gone. She smoked cigarettes. She wore lipstick and stuff on her eyes, she smelled of perfume, she confessed carelessly that she wouldn't know how to change a plug, let alone rewire a house (this was what Graham's mother had done in the cottage, the previous summer).

One night, the last of Claudia's family's stay, there was a very high tide: the whole flat sandy bottom of the valley they usually walked down to reach the beach was flooded with the sea. They made a bonfire, cooked sausages and potatoes, and took it in turns to take a rowing boat out on the water. It was shallow and calm, they had to watch out for the current where the river flowed, but his mother didn't believe in overprotecting them. The water that night was full of phosphorescence, tiny sea-creatures that glowed in the dark: an enzyme-catalyzed chemical reaction, their father told them.

Graham took Claudia out in the boat with her daughters: she sat opposite him while he rowed, the two little girls cuddled on either side of her, hushed and still for once. Every time he lifted the oars out of the water they dripped with liquid light in the darkness, and where the oars dropped into the water they made bright holes and ripples of light went racing out from them. In the dark Claudia took her feet out of her shoes and put them on his. He was rowing in bare feet, he'd left his flip-flops on the sand. He rowed up and down, his stroke faultless, in a kind of trance, until eventually the others were shouting for them from the shore.

– Come on, you idiot! Don't hog the boat! Give someone else a go!

And all the time she was rubbing her feet up and down his, he could feel the thick calloused skin on her heels and on the ball of her foot, her splayed brown toes and the hard polish of her nails, the sand she ground against him, that stuck to their ankles and calves in the wet bottom of the boat.

Then the next day she went, and he suffered. For the first time like an adult, secretly.

More than twenty years later when Graham had children of his own he saw Claudia again. The sixth-form college he taught at was sometimes hired out for functions out of school hours: one Friday when he'd had to stay late for a meeting he met the delegates for some conference coming in as he left. His glance fell on the board in the foyer: a course on Food Hygiene. The woman who came up the front steps directly at him, her conference folder hugged across her chest, chatting with assurance to a friend, was stouter, and smarter (her buttons all did up), and her hair was a shining even grey cut in a shoulder-length bob. But it was unmistakably her: the pugnacious jaw, the upturned nose, the loose wide mouth. These things about her he'd forgotten for decades suddenly reconnected themselves into the unmistakable stamp of her.

The moment she had passed, he doubted it. He was hallucinating, some chance feature of a stranger had triggered a memory he hadn't known he'd kept. He turned and saw her disappearing through the double doors. Then another woman with a folder came running up the steps towards him, looking past him: she'd seen someone she knew.

– Claudia! she called. And the grey-haired woman turned.

That night when his wife came in from seeing a film with her girlfriends, brash and defensive from her couple of drinks in the Arts Centre bar, he told her about Claudia. He had been sitting marking a pile of school folders, he saw her take in the mugs with black coffee dregs left on the desk as if they were reproachful reminders of his austerity and dutifulness. His *puritanism*, she called it.

He wasn't sure why he told her about Claudia now. Carol had insisted years ago on confessing all her experiences with men, but he hadn't really wanted to know, not out of jealousy but real indifference: how could these things be shared? But she leaned across him to collect the mugs and he caught the blare of wine on her breath: he imagined that she'd been complaining about him as usual to Rose and Fran, that the only things he ever got excited about were quantum mechanics and quarks. Then he suddenly felt as if he had cheated her out of some knowledge of himself without which she was vulnerable.

He told her when they were lying in bed together in the dark. She didn't like his story. At first she didn't believe it.

– Oh, but Gray! You were just fantasising! Why would a grown-up sensible woman want . . .

Then she got up and put on the light, sat down at the dressing table and creamed her face; briskly and matter of factly as if she'd forgotten to do it before she came to bed, working cream in with her fingertips against the downwards droop, concentrating angrily on her reflection.

– But what would you think if you heard about this . . . If you heard about a *man*, doing this to a thirteen-year-old girl, to your own daughter, to Hannah, what would you think? It's *horrible*.

He didn't tell her that he'd seen Claudia again.

He found out her address quite easily, by telephoning the conference organisers. He went to the house twice in his lunch hour when there was no one there. It was tucked away down a little mews street, a square Georgian house with a modern glassy extension: when he peered inside he could see Turkish rugs on a tiled floor, abstract paintings on the walls, a huge white paper globe for a lampshade. He checked the address on his piece of paper to be sure it was really hers: everything about the house was quietly wealthy, far beyond the reach of a laboratory technician, or even a university lecturer.

The third time he went after school and there was a plum-coloured old Jaguar parked in the courtyard under the flowering cherry, a few petals scattered on its bonnet. Claudia answered the door. She was dressed in a batik-printed kimono and he could smell the smoke from the cigarette she had just put down.

– Claudia? It's Graham Cooley.

She was perfectly blank, searched her memory half-heartedly, accepting the hand he put out.

– It's a long time ago. You came on holiday with us, stayed in our chalet in West Wales.

– Oh: *Cooley!* A *long* time ago! Goodness me! I do remember, I think. That family with all the boys. Which one were you? But that was in another lifetime! How extraordinary. And of course you're grown-up.

She still didn't make that movement from the door which would invite him in: she was stubbornly guarding whatever little ritual of peace and privacy he had interrupted. Close to, he could see where the skin was loosening to hang under her jaw, and the eyes sun-crinkled from too many tans.

He insisted. With obvious misgivings – what ever did he *want?* – and finding it difficult even to remember anything

7

about his mother and father to make conversation out of, she let him in and made him coffee and sat him in the glass room in a chair made of blond wood and tubular chrome opposite hers. The coffee was good, strong espresso.

– So what have you done with yourself then, Graham? she said. You were an awfully talented family, weren't you? Terrifying. What about your brothers? Were you the third? Tim, wasn't it, and Paul?

– Not Paul, he said, Philip. I was the fourth. He reached across – the chrome chair although it looked awkward was comfortable and supportive – and put his hand heavily on her leg above the knee. She had put on a lot of weight, she was really very solid between bust and hips, but her flesh was compact and warm. – *Don't* you remember? Really?

She froze. She was looking at him horrified, at first only thinking, whoever is he, how to get him out of here, why ever did I let him in, against my better judgement? But then as he searched her eyes something behind them burst, some containing membrane, and then what she remembered spread through her, filling her, making her skin flush deeper and deeper, making her body sag and yield, filling her eyes with water even. – Oh, yes, she said. Oh . . . Oh, so you *did* know. Oh, God, I suppose I'd managed to convince myself afterwards that you wouldn't have noticed, that it had just been my own fantasy . . . And then, just now, I simply forgot, I'd forgotten all about it, it's years since I've thought about that summer . . .

– You do remember?

– Well, something awful. I really thought though, you wouldn't have guessed, that it was all just my own horrible idea.

– But in the boat . . .

– In the boat? In the boat? What did I do in the boat? Oh,

don't tell me, please, I don't want to know. God – I can't explain it, there's no explanation. When my own son got to that age I used to think, that boy . . . It was such a rotten summer, Don and I . . . I remember I used to sit there on the beach just dreaming of lacerating him all over with a kitchen knife. Poor Don. He really wasn't so bad. Cooped up all summer together in that awful hut . . . She looked at him with shock. – You do know that Don and I split up? No, of course, why should you? But that was in another lifetime, really . . . My husband's an architect. We had another daughter together, four children altogether . . . She spelled out these things as if she owed him explanations.

– Are the children at school?

– At school? Her eyes were wet again, her loose mouth slipped, smiling, she took his hand off her knee. – I'm a grandmother. I've got two grandchildren. The daughter you didn't know – she's at Art College, final year. You see – I'm an old woman. Hideous, isn't it? Oh God, this is awful. Let's have a drink.

She poured them both huge splashes of Scotch.

– But your name's the same, that's how I followed you up.

– I didn't want all that business – taking my husband's name. I wanted to do things differently, the second time. Whether it worked out so very different, this man woman thing, it's so difficult . . .

They chinked glasses, she blushed very darkly. – Have you *forgiven* me? It hasn't ruined your life or anything? I'm really so ashamed. I was, afterwards, then I began to wonder if I really could have done anything so awful. I thought I might have just dreamed it. But of course I've never thought I'd see you, that we'd recognise one another. We lived in the north for years.

– I recognised you. Why Food Hygiene, by the way?

She was blank again. – Oh! Food Hygiene! She ran mentally over a room of faces. – Were you at that conference? Yes, I part-own a restaurant, a French restaurant in Kingswell.

They drank their whisky quickly and she poured more with shaking hands. She looked appeasingly into his face. – You *are* nice-looking, she said. I always had good taste in men. Oh dear. It *is* alright, isn't it? You haven't come to punish me or anything?

– God, no, he said. That's the last thing.

None the less when he began kissing her and putting his hands under her clothes he did it without tentativeness, as if he was claiming something he was owed. And she let him, watched him, said, – Are you really sure? I don't think of anyone wanting this from me any more. I mean, any stranger.

– I'm not a stranger, he said.

– You are to me, she said. In spite of everything you tell me. I remember it, just. But of course not with you. I remember a boy, you see. I've never seen you before.

But she didn't stop him. Several times, for all his intentness, he caught her look of curiosity at him, curiosity like his own, hard and greedy and tinged with shame.

Carol swung the door open at his ring, red faced.

– Where have you been? I've been out of my mind. I've phoned all the hospitals, your dinner's ruined, the kids . . .

– Oh God, didn't I tell you? We had a GCSE moderation, it went on for bloody hours. I'm sure I told you. I said I'd get sandwiches.

– But I phoned the college, there was no answer.

– Carol, love, I'm sorry . . . The phone rings in the office, there's no one there to pick it up. I'm *sorry*, maybe I did forget to mention it. I was so sure I had. Let me come in and get the kids to bed for you.

She stood staring at him. – It's so unlike you. You're usually so organised. But I really don't remember you telling me about this one. And isn't it a bit early for a moderation? You haven't finished marking all the papers yet.

For a moment he was sure she could smell something on him, see something of the great dazzle that was clinging to him, dripping off him, flashing round in his veins. But he saw her deliberately tidy that intimation away, out of consciousness. This was her husband, the man she knew. He was a physics teacher and a competition-standard chess player, wasn't he?

CHALKING THE STONE

~

Alexandra Ward

They met at a Miners' Rally. Her roots were in the South Wales coalfield, his in the North of England. A bit of a mixed marriage you might say. There is a photograph of them, the only one of them together, which must have been taken about that time. She in a pale summer frock. He in a shiny suit too small for him. They look awkward, shoulder to shoulder, head to head, hands clasped, by order of the photographer. He, as if he had just smiled but failed to hold the unfamiliar expression, and she, well like she always looks, shy and a bit miffed at the same time. The photograph, lopsided in its cheap frame, stands beside the alarm clock on the mantelpiece. I can see her now, dusting. Up goes the frame in her left hand, swipe, swipe, beneath it with her right. And down it goes again, and never a glance at it, never a secret smile of recollection or regret.

That photograph of my Mam and Dad. You would hardly recognise them. Not because they looked younger then, which they did, or happier, which they did not, but because they seemed so ordinary and undifferentiated. Whereas now they look as if they are carved out of some gritty acidic stone. Monuments to some fearful forgotten battle, the dates, the names effaced by relentless weathering. I only ever saw her laugh but once, I mean really gut-renderingly laugh, and that was at a church social a long time ago. She was in a group of women setting out the tea. One of them made some joke about the jellies. You could tell it was vulgar. They were making them wobble, and laughing, all of them, tears running down their cheeks, my mother wiping her eyes, laughing. But I've never seen my father laugh. Never.

Not that it mattered. They had their own separate zones of influence, their own lives quite distinct from each other. His was centred on the pit and the club. He wasn't a drinker. He could make a pint last all evening. He was an observer. Sitting at one of the long tables with his back to the wall, watching the pool, watching the darts, listening. Not saying much. Not even thinking perhaps. You could never tell. Yes, they had reached an understanding.

But understanding is not enough. It is necessary but not sufficient. His hands started to go funny. They'd get the shakes for no reason. The fingertips would go white. Like Raynaud's, the doctor said. An identifiable disease. Vibration white finger. It was the cutting machinery, see. The doctor explained it all. The symptoms, sometimes tingling, sometimes dead, always shaking. The useless white fingers. It was all caused by spasm in the small arteries. You understand, the doctor said. Yes, my father said. Yes, my mother said. They understood. He was out of work, yes? The doctor wrote him off.

At first, he couldn't stop getting up at the old time, and the day hung about him long and as useless as his hands. Then he got to staying in bed. She got up as she always did. Worked through her chores. Ignored him as much as she could, as if by doing so she could banish him back to the pit and make things normal again. In a way it was better when he got up late. He wasn't under her feet. But it wasn't that simple. She still knew he was there, somewhere, in the house, and it made her feel uneasy, unsettled, invaded.

She couldn't stand to see his hands shaking either. He knew it too. Tried to keep them hidden, but it only made things worse. Trouble was there was nowhere for him to go during the day and he no longer went to the club in the evening. Nor did anyone seek him out. On dry days he'd go up the mountain. Take some snap in his pocket and stay out all day. But even that didn't suit her. She said it was like having a kid about the place, only turning up for meals, and then not staying to wash up. Well he couldn't could he, I mean not with white finger? She knew it too, but she couldn't leave it alone. They were like a couple who had settled out of court but who still had unfinished business.

I'd come upon my Dad holding out his hands in front of him, like a drunk trying to prove to himself that he is sober. Whenever my Mam caught him at it he'd shove his hands in his pockets and try to look casual, something he had never been at any time in his life. It made her so angry. She'd start banging the poker about in the hearth, and he'd retaliate with 'What you want to go and make all that mess for?' Though he knew why right enough. It was the custom of her country. When the fire was fitful, it meant the Devil had got in it, and you had to poke and rattle away at the fire until you drove him out. And then to keep him out, you chalked all these intricate patterns from one side of the hearth to the other. A sort of fancy fence. It always frightened me, the rattling. But what scared me most was not the thought of the Devil loose in the house, so much as what might happen if he had already slipped back past the earlier faded defences, the paled plaits, and into the fire and couldn't get out. The thought of the Devil trapped in our hearth, trapped and getting angrier by the minute terrified me.

When he finally escaped, it was a relief, like the sudden giving way of a slip knot. 'Diawl, I can't get this bloody thing to light,' she said. 'Come out you little bugger.' She kept poking at it, poking at it, not giving it a chance. 'Let me have a go,' my Dad said, trying to ease in beside her, take over for once. Nothing to break here. But she held her ground and her face was screwed up, spiteful looking. 'Magic powers, is it? Fancy you can keep the home fires burning? Joke.' She was going to go on in that vein for some time, you could see. She'd worked herself up to it chasing the Devil. But he spun her round and slapped her across the mouth, quick like. So quick it was almost as if you had imagined it. But you hadn't. His white finger marks blossomed into strawberry-mark red ones on her face. He'd never hit her before, never hit anyone. It wasn't his style. It was awful. Ugly. What should have been a place of solace and respite had become a cage for the desperate and the ill-spirited, a place of acute danger.

She turned away from him, knelt down and with shaking hands began sweeping the hearth. He watched, immobilised by shock and shame and the knowledge that not all his anger had been expended, that one blow would never be enough. 'You've got a steady enough hand when you want,' she said. It was a statement. He looked down at his hands, the old habit. They were taut shiny purple-blue claws, but steady, unrepentant. Whatever he did, she would always block him. He side-stepped her, left her kneeling. The cheap loud tock of the alarm clock shocked him. Alarmed he knew it was time to go.

Suddenly the fire kindled. Flames were running through the coals, exploring the spaces between. Her back was to me. She went on sweeping the hearth. Moving everything back so that the slate was a bare rectangle in the glow from the fire. Then she put her hand in her apron pocket and withdrew a piece of chalk she kept there for the purpose and she began drawing a knot garden of whirls, spirals, interlacing lines all over the hearth. Usually, she did a fairly simple braid of interwoven lines from one side of the hearth to the other, just enough to stop the Devil getting through, sneaking back, no more. But this time she really went to town, until a regular Book of Kells was revealed. She was not taking any chances. She was still on her knees scratching away, chalk nearly gone, when he came downstairs, heavy boots thudding, thudding on bare wood, then clacking, clacking on bare stone, and out through the door. No change of pace. No hesitation.

At the sound of the door slamming shut Mam got off her knees and wiped her fingers on her apron. But she couldn't seem to get the chalk off, and she kept on wiping them, wiping them, until they were raw red, even after, as far as I could see, the chalk and her reason for using it was long gone.

CATWOMEN FROM HELL

~

Kitty Sewell

A trickle of sweat tickled the middle of my back. I was wearing black leathers (straining alarmingly at the seams) from top to bottom. Underneath this, granny knickers and full-length woolly thermals. Also, my mum's hand-knitted roll-neck Cowichan wool sweater and two pairs of socks.

On the table, my sinister black helmet. Next to the helmet, a pint of dark liquid, luke warm and slightly frothing. (Why, I asked myself, when I liked a fine glass of chilled white wine, possibly a vodka on ice splashed with merely a breath of martini.)

I was sitting in a corner of The Mouse and Rat in Swansea, a drinking establishment not for the faint-hearted. This was precisely the reason I was there, in the act of defying the encroachment of middle age and taking a bold leap into the unknown. Forty had come and gone with much knuckle-biting and angst. Having weathered this milestone, what could I possibly do which would – in a big way – put a halt to the creeping, nay galloping, passage of time? The solution: a large, fast and ostentatiously decorated motorcycle. Type: Harley Davidson (but not quite the real thing).

This bike of mine was parked outside in the street, gleaming in the bright spring sun, its genuine, politically incorrect crocodile-skin panniers shining with layers of beeswax polish. The matching tool-kit strapped to the handle-bars filled, not with spanners, but lipstick, hair brush and compact mirror.

I shouldn't fail to mention the unbelievable challenge of

having learned to ride this thing and then, on a cold March morning when it had the gall to snow, taking my riding test.

At the sight of me, the examiner was understandably baffled and stumped for words. He fitted a one-way receiver to my helmet and ordered me to hit the road where he followed at a safe distance in his car, barking out instructions through a crackling intercom. Seeing that I had spent the entire winter practising and had faithfully attended the Sunday morning riding classes, offered by kindly and elderly motorbike enthusiasts (all men of course), he could not but give me an exemplary pass. I had perfected the fine art of hill starts and emergency stops. I was ready and on the brink of immortality.

But why stop there? I placed an advert in the *South Wales Evening Post* reading: 'Women on big fast bikes (500cc minimum, no kid's stuff) wishing to find like-minded, meet at the Mouse and Rat, 2pm Saturday.'

And thus, here I was. I checked my watch again, 2:27, and I was still on my own, scrutinized with both sniggers and some admiration by the all-male clientele, some of whom had seen the magnificent beast parked outside and, noticing my gear, put two and forty-two together. Nevertheless, the spotlight was uncomfortable and I deplored the cowardice of women bikers not to come forward at my selfless summons. The warm bitter liquid had gone to my head a bit and I was swearing silently, I'm obviously the only effing woman rider in the whole of South Bloody Wales, when a very large woman in tattered brown leathers strode in.

When our eyes met, we were equally embarrassed. It can take all of two seconds to totally take in another person and the difference between us was instantly noted. I wished to God that I'd gone easy on the make-up, and I figured that the bike on which this woman had arrived was not gleaming but spattered with mud and cow shit and sporting many rusting scrapes and dents. She had already seen my bike and would have drawn her own conclusion.

Our awkward acquaintance did not last for long. Shortly two more women came in, helmets wedged in armpits, furtively glancing about in the dim bar. I waved a tad too cheerfully and the two approached looking thoroughly suspicious. I deemed them to be romantically linked, a fact that did not seem to sit well with the large woman whose name was Siân. As Brenda and Mick returned to our table with their pints, Siân resolutely turned her back to stare at something above the bar.

We were saved from further mortification by the arrival of a fairly normal-looking woman whose name was Helen. She was a psychiatric nurse in a local hospital. Aside from the helmet she was dressed as if setting off on a hearty ramble, hiking boots, sensible waterproof trousers and a Goretex jacket. A tidy backpack held further sound provisions, I imagined, such as a flask of hot tea, fig rolls and tissues. Her Diet Coke in front of her, she enquired politely about our various professions and marital status.

Siân was a farmer's wife, whose husband at her insistence had abandoned sheep in favour of horses. He was, she said, not a happy man since horse breeding was not lucrative or easy, especially since he knew little about it. She loved horses more than people, she claimed bitterly, and the rest of us shifted uncomfortably in our seats. I could picture her massive thighs astride just about anything, bikes, horses and the disgruntled husband, who apparently had little say in any matter. Trying to dismiss this image I heard Mick saying that she and Brenda were into pyramid sales and were hoping to buy a remote cottage in France one day.

– You can buy one for about five grand, chirped Brenda

whose voice was surprisingly melodious considering her cropped hair and menacing demeanour.

– No one would fucking bother us there, said Mick whose angry voice, again, was in conflict with her slight and delicate build.

I was reluctantly about to own up to my well-heeled and ordered life, and was saved from it by the entrance of an unusual person. She was tiny, more like a miniature woman of indeterminable age. Her gorgeous attire was a brilliant white leather suit with long fringes which swayed gracefully in unison with her long glossy red hair. I instantly stopped worrying about my lipstick and silk scarf and noted with envy the glamour of this Lilliputian but totally self-assured individual. There was much nudging and drooling at the bar. Mick sniggered and glanced at Brenda, whose eyes, like all in the room, were riveted on the woman. She flashed us a brilliant smile and sashayed up to the bar to get, damn it, a vodka martini.

My role felt quite unfortunately like that of a hostess, since no one else was about to perform introductions or in any way broach the subject of why we were all here together.

– I've gathered you all here before me today, I began in mock ceremony but my joke was not well received, or possibly misunderstood and I suddenly experienced a massive hot flush. The homeopathic stuff's gotta go, I thought grimly and resolved to get a prescription for some proper hormones on Monday.

India, the new woman, exuded the heady aroma of Dune and on closer inspection her immaculately made-up face was possibly even older than mine. Thank the Lord, someone as antique, and even more conspicuous. I was dying to know what sort of bike she rode, and I was not to be disappointed. How a tiny thing like her could manage a proper Harley I would have to see for myself.

It was close to four when the last biker woman appeared, already the worse for wear from some other rendezvous. She was quite a sight. Her neck and hands had many mismatched tattoos, most of them home-made, and her face was pierced here and there by rings and studs, even a chip of wood and a sliver of bone. Not a bit self-conscious she stared at each of us in turn, her hands loosely on her skinny hips, a half smoked roll-up glued to her lower lip. We all fell mute under her scrutiny. She laughed from somewhere deep in her throat and as if to make up for the intrusion she offered to buy us all a drink. Our collective eyes were on stalks when she pulled an amazingly large wad of twenty pound notes from her tattered jean jacket.

– What are we doing then? said she, her name was Tania, and slapped Mick hard on the back making the table and the drinks rattle dangerously. Mick shot her a filthy look but said nothing.

– I had in mind some sort of club, I started. Tania looked at me for a long moment with a smirk and then turned to the others.

– Who's she? she jerked her thumb in my direction.

I cringed and wished myself far away, such as in a nice wine bar with my agreeable friends. Perspiration continued its relentless march down my body and I tugged at my mum's scratchy roll-neck with mounting claustrophobia.

The discussion nevertheless turned to the aims of our meeting and the idea of a club was not unwelcome. In spite of our differences we became excited and animated, like kids, plotting our club and its intentions. What to name it?

– How about Swansea Lady Riders? I ventured. A nice respectable name that would stand the test of time.

A shriek of sarcastic mirth from Tania convinced me what a sad fucker I was. Helen the nurse suggested Women on

Wheels, the WOWs, for short. This was mulled over at length. No, even this was too tame.

The Welsh She Wolves? – too much of a tongue-twister.

The Real Hell's Angels? – risk of agitating rival gangs, but we were getting hotter.

– The CatWomen from Hell, cried out Brenda in her dulcet voice, and a pregnant silence fell as we all looked at each other.

– Yes! Sorted! we all shouted and banged our hands on the table spilling drinks and attracting some nervous glances from the bar. If I was going to beat the menopause, how better than as a CatWoman from Hell.

But there were more tough decisions to make. What were to be the aims and activities of the CatWomen? We all put forward a suggestion.

– Fortnightly rides, I submitted cautiously.

– Run over stray sheep, shouted Tania.

– Scare old ladies, giggled Brenda.

– Rob banks, said Mick seriously.

– Drink beer and talk about bikes, proposed Siân.

– Do sponsored charity rides, suggested Helen sensibly.

We all looked at India, waiting to hear her proposal. She smiled cryptically and studied her long red fingernails.

– I know where the Black Riders meet . . .

– NO WAY! we all shouted unanimously – no bloody men.

– Fraternizing with male bikers will be against the rules of this society on pain of pulled out fingernails, asserted Siân, staring intently at India's manicured hands which quickly disappeared into tight white leather pockets.

As if on cue, a man came through the door pulling off his helmet and looking around with interest. He advanced towards us with a puzzled look on his face. The poor guy had obviously seen the bikes outside and quite rightly taken it for a meet.

– Hey, stop right there, shouted Tania.

– Get lost, added Siân.

– Fuck off, joined in Mick and Brenda aggressively.

Myself, India and Helen looked at him and shrugged our shoulders apologetically, not without regret. He was a delectable specimen, tall and slim, a peculiar yet beautiful face. His leathers were tidy and his thick shoulder-length hair perfectly clean. But at this crude rejection the attractive man slunk out of the door with as much dignity as he could muster, followed by the jeers of the guys at the bar. Well, as we said, no fraternizing.

An hour or so later we all spilled out into the sun, squinting and in various states of drunkenness. The bikes were all lined up nicely as if we already knew what we were doing. The inevitable comparisons singled me and India out as the rich bitches, not just rich but conceited, not proper bikers. Helen had a sensible no-frills Honda 500. Siân a massive Yamaha of some 1500cc, and the rest a variety of greasy rat-bikes of unrecognizable origins. Convulsions of laughter, shouting, bad language and insults were flying about. Tania was seriously getting on my nerves with her sarky comments and I was starting to wonder what sort of monster I had created.

Our first ride a week later was a nightmare of dizzy speeds and everyone trying to overtake everyone else. Who said that women are not competitive? For some of those ladies, no risk was big enough when it came to outdoing her fellow riders. I was still a total novice and for a time I resigned myself to being the slow-poke and the kill-joy, to the constant taunts and hilarity of Tania the Terror. Her scorn did in fact help by pissing me off to a degree where I forced myself to get more proficient.

We met faithfully once a fortnight and all entered into the spirit of revolt and rampage with equal enthusiasm. A decree was drawn up that no new member could join without first submitting to an elaborate initiation ritual, consisting of many outrageous, embarrassing and unhealthy acts. No one else joined.

Many rides later, notoriety followed. Old ladies scarpered and children cried when they saw us roaring down the street, sans silencers. Men laughed, but nervously. The CatWomen from Hell made a motley bunch. We looked scary, we were scary. We made the Hell's Angels look like toddlers in nappies and bonnets riding forth in frilly prams, or so we fancied. People parted quickly to make way for us in pubs, and when we lounged outside on the grass with our pints and raucous laughter, mothers would scurry off with their little children to save them from our noxious influence.

As a group we couldn't agree on anything, and any type of manifesto could not be compiled without the risk of fisticuffs, yet we had something in common and it bound us together. Bar robbing banks, we did all the things we had set out to do, and more. I foresaw my whole middle age as a spree of roaring around the hills, hell raising, drinking and fighting.

I fell off my bike a number of times and soon it too was scratched and greasy and my leathers dirty and scuffed. I learned a large repertoire of filthy words, had a go at snorting some white powdery stuff and let my fingernails get dirty. My CatWoman persona was allowed to laugh at smutty jokes and racist remarks, snarl at children and dogs, spit, fart and smoke – all the things my other self abhorred. Once in a cheerful brawl when Tania called me a posh twat, I acciden-tally gave her a black eye and she came away with a handful of my precious golden locks (which were already thinning somewhat in spite of the HRT). Ah, what did it matter? We made up again and Tania gave me her cherished rabbit foot and I gave her my silk Harley Davidson scarf which she subsequently kept tied around her thigh. We were sexy, we were raunchy, we were it.

– Mum, why don't you take your lot over Port Talbot way, or Carmarthenshire, or the valleys, pleaded Elise, my daughter. She and her friends had run into us outside Joe's ice-cream parlour, and to her I was not sexy, cool, or it. Just a mastodonic mega-embarrassment.

– Darling, you must be careful, said my medical husband, surveying the dents on my petrol tank. He was such a tolerant man I decided to shave my armpits and scrub my nails of an evening. He was still on the good wines whereas I had graduated to Guinness, an attempt to work my way through the warm flat liquids to find one that I could actually stomach (Guinness turned out to be 400 calories a pint, so it too had to go). He even put up with my smoking, although barred me from lighting up in the bedroom where, incidentally, things had taken an interesting turn for the better.

By day I was still the respectable psychotherapist and few people at work knew of my alter ego. When alone in my consulting room I took to hissing and scratching at the air as a way of reminding myself that I was more than I seemed. My professional analysis of this behaviour exposed a dark side of my nature. A long repressed sub-personality was baring its teeth and I had no choice but to roar. Hidden within the recesses of my psyche was a wild woman, whose murky desires commanded me with no regard for convention or decorum. The symbol of this not-yet-totally unleashed madness was the cat. It wasn't for nothing that my name was Kitty.

These thoughts and ruminations occupied my mind in

between unsuspecting clients. All they saw was a neat and tidy professional woman with a practical, no-nonsense approach to the crises and predicaments of life.

Tania's second name was Trouble and within eight months of the birth of the CatWomen she got into trouble with the law. She wouldn't say exactly, but the wads of cash she carried about with her undoubtedly had something to do with it. Gradually she stopped making her late appearances and we stopped waiting for her. Nobody knew where she lived or who it was that left bruises on her arms and neck. She really had been a closed book. I was left with the rabbit foot as a memento of the woman who had taught me a vocabulary that no university could rival.

A few months later Mick and Brenda fell out, first with each other then with the CatWomen. Pyramid sales had been lean, their beloved Spaniel had died a long and painful death and the stress was showing. Brenda had an eye for the girls, particularly India. India was a naughty sort and had encouraged this interest just for the hell of it, for which she received a bruised nose courtesy of Mick.

Mick took to wearing her Walkman so she could listen to Conversational French, Ten Easy Lessons, partly to shut us out and partly to learn French. She soon set off on her bike with her panniers loaded and a pocket full of dosh to purchase the longed for cottage in Normandy. She always was a loner anyway and seemed just as happy going solo. We gave her a good send-off and henceforth Brenda became even more gregarious and personable. She grew her hair and started singing in a band. In a flash this band really took off and Brenda got swept up into a whole new life, far away from pyramid sales and CatWomen. In our honour she wrote a song about her biking days, but she no longer had time for us. Her bike fell by the wayside, literally.

The departure of those three took the sting out of the CatWomen somewhat. Problem now was that Siân and India couldn't stand each other. One was as vast as the other was minute (sixteen stone to six). One as coarse as the other dainty. I found myself reverting to counselling mode and attempting to mediate, to sooth. Sensible Helen, also of psychiatric background, told me to let them battle it out. Battle they did, but in a catty, not Catwomanish, way. The bickering was boring and it dawned on me: we were no longer mad, bad or dangerous.

I quit the fags and a near crash made me resolve never ever to drink and ride. India and I discussed our purchases in the sales and Helen drank tea out of her flask and compiled to-do lists in a little notebook. Siân grunted and complained, and once we had to suffer the indignity of the presence of two brats (she'd never confessed to them before), one of whom spilled a milkshake over my genuine, politically incorrect, crocodile seat covers.

One Saturday when Siân was waylaid by her discontented and overworked husband, India, Helen and I felt the need to resurrect some of the rebelliousness that had brought us together. What naughty thing could we get up to? With manhating Siân out of the way we quickly hatched a plot. The treachery of this dreadful scheme and the scornful disregard for our treaty got us all into a state of high excitement. We set off at high speeds toward the notorious Blooming Rose, the meeting place of the Black Riders. It was our best and fastest ride yet. As we drew up to the vast parking green of the Rose, we were greeted by a sea of bikes and the men that rode them. I prayed I wouldn't topple my heavy machine as I parked it in full view of this mass (this was known to happen when I was under observation).

We were instantly surrounded by hordes of curious males.

I cannot remember, even in the flush of youth, having had so much splendid attention. It was a sunny spring day, birds sang, the grass was green and the beer flowed. Spring has this drug-like effect on bike enthusiasts, they become boisterous, no, demented. I found and flirted wildly with Rhisiart, the hapless intruder of our first meeting, and even Helen was seen sitting on the knee of a bearded Kris Kristofferson lookalike. But India took the cake, she was as shameless a hussy as any CatWoman could ever hope to be. Helen and I watched anxiously as she homed in on the most interesting looking men, girlfriends notwithstanding. Predictably, she got into a fierce slanging-match with one of these women on account of some unwise comment about wimps who ride pillion behind their men. She mostly got away with these things because of her tiny stature, no one with a speck of honour would lay into someone that small. The burly boyfriend in question was so smitten he lifted her up and tossed and twirled her around his head for several minutes. She claimed to have been a trapeze artist and now I believed her, it was clearly true. The whole spectacle was very graceful and people cheered and bought us drinks.

We didn't know it at the time, but this flirt-fest was the last proper escapade of our ever-diminishing band. Not long after, India mysteriously found herself pregnant. She couldn't believe it. She was mid-forties and had been told long ago that her tubes were gummed-up and she would never have the pleasure of brats. She definitely was not the motherly type, and the alleged father was even less so, but the miracle of the conception dissuaded her from asking any searching questions of herself, and soon her little body had a bump on the front of it. Riding Harleys was now regarded as a dangerous pastime. An excellent CatWoman lost to bikehood.

Siân was more and more held hostage by hostile hubby

to help with the horses and housewifery, so finally our fear-less gang was reduced to good old Helen and myself. Our sedate rides and mugs of tea on top of panoramic hills were pleasant enough, but even they fizzled out as Helen got a promotion. Nursing claimed the soul of this extremely nice but hopelessly responsible lady. Yet another CatWoman bit the dust.

EPILOGUE

On the bleak moors of Wales a lone hunched rider in black can sometimes be seen. In the ghostly whirls of the dawn mists or in the eerie stillness of dusk, blood-curdling cat-calls can be heard echoing over the hills. An unearthly rumble of engine fading into the darkness of night, fused with the wailing of winds.

From here until the end of time, in body or in spirit, there will always be one true CatWoman from Hell.

I am the last of my kind.

SNAKESKIN BECOMES HER

~

Jo Hughes

What Jessica wants is to be cured of her incurable sadness. She's walking through town gazing in shop windows and going through rack after rack of clothing looking for a cure. Maybe she's looking for herself. She picks up a long flowered dress, studies it, then asks herself, 'Is this me?' She wistfully fingers a pair of pink satin trousers and runs her hand over a tiny mohair sweater that has a little red silk heart sewn over the bosom – 'Is this me?'

Maybe sackcloth would be the thing. Or a polyester frock with someone else's sweat stains straining at the armpits and an old wig, stiff and dun coloured. And plastic leather-look shoes and American Tan tights. Maybe that would be a true reflection of who Jessica is.

Tonight she has a date and that's the reason for this flurry of activity. I have a date, she thinks as she withdraws money from the bank. Money she knows she shouldn't be spending.

'I have a date!' she says aloud in the chemist's as she buys mouthwash and a small bottle of her favourite scent, 'Poison'. When she says aloud, 'I have a date!' the assistant is supposed to smile, but instead she just stares at Jessica, stony-faced.

Unnerved by this, Jessica goes for a coffee and tries to inspire herself by looking at a fashion magazine. A song is playing on the radio; a hit from a year or so ago. To Jessica it seems to belong to another age, to the time of her youth and innocence. The time before her heart got broken. Not again, she thinks, frowning at the doe-eyed model's face on the glossy page before her, *never* again.

She smiles ruefully, adds more sugar to her coffee and turns to the horoscope page. Still humming the song, she drains her cup of its last sweet dregs, then wanders out to the next shop. Once there she chooses five dresses, all of them short and clinging, and enters the changing room. She quickly undresses, then tries on the one which is made from a print of silvery snakeskin. She can't decide whether she looks wonderful or absurd in it. She strikes a casual pose, then an artificial, angular one, then she tries to catch a glimpse of her reflection from behind to see if her bottom looks too big. Finally she unzips herself and lets the dress slither like a dead thing to her ankles.

After three hours of shopping Jessica begins to feel panic rise up in her. She should be feeling the beginnings of transformation. She should feel like Cinderella before the ball, but the rats are still rats and the pumpkin remains the same. She would swear that the money in her bag is getting heavier. She's drunk too much coffee and hasn't eaten and her heart is pounding. The day has grown darker and seagulls now reel and scream overhead as they make their way inland dragging a storm in their wake.

The voice inside her, which earlier had been happily pronouncing, 'I've got a date! A date!' has subtly attached a question mark to itself. Why is she calling it a date? Why the word which conjures images of neatly-combed young men in tweed sports coats who clear their throats awkwardly and loosen their collars in cliched gestures? It is the language of hot kisses and noses bumping instead of the one she intends to speak.

She walks on, her knees beginning to feel weak. Sadness is taking hold of her and her last piece of hope is diminishing. She remembers a weather house she'd had as a child. She thinks about the little figure with the umbrella and its miserable expression as it swung out of one door while the other figure retreated with her basket of flowers into the shadows.

Then suddenly she is confronted by a familiar face. It is smiling and saying brightly, 'Jessica! Jessica!'

Jessica, still half submerged in her reverie, makes a weak attempt at a returning smile.

'How *are* you? Oh, it's been ages! How are things?'

The speaker is Vivien, a woman whom Jessica has known vaguely for years. Jessica manages to mutter something in reply about not feeling too good.

'Oh, me too. I've got a dreadful cold.' Vivien sneezes then as if to prove it and after wiping her nose continues, 'You've just missed Brian. What a pity! He'll be sorry he missed you.'

It is strange to hear his name out loud like that, Jessica thinks, almost indecent. It was a name she'd only thought about in whispers. She imagines him strolling up the road – maybe even walking right past her and the two of them not noticing each other. She thinks of how he'd have thrown his head back in a delighted laugh if he'd seen her, and of how he would have hugged her close to him, close enough to smell the damp wool and stale tobacco smell of his coat.

She remembers his voice from that morning; the husky half-asleep way he'd said hello when he'd picked up the phone, the sigh of longing in his every word.

Vivien chats away – Jessica has always envied Vivien's ability to make conversation. But Jessica isn't really listening. She is thinking about Brian with his arms around her waist, his lips on hers. She forces herself to listen, to focus and respond. Vivien says '. . . so Brian threw a surprise party for my thirtieth birthday!'

Jessica laughs and nods politely at this, but inside she thinks, Thirty! She can't believe it. But then she's always known that Vivien is older than Brian and he's twenty five.

Jessica herself is a few weeks short of her twentieth birthday. She stares at Vivien's face closely.

Thirty. How can Brian bear it? How can Vivien bear it? No wonder Brian wants to see Jessica tonight. And yet Vivien *is* beautiful. Tall and slender and pale-skinned with something ballerina-like about her face, especially when her dark hair is drawn tightly back as it is now.

Vivien studies Jessica. She doesn't much like her, but doesn't actually dislike her either. It is generally agreed among their circle of friends that Jessica is a little unhinged. As Vivien watches she notices how Jessica has a strange nervous tic; a habit of flicking out her tongue and moistening her upper lip. Vivien remembers what Brian had said that morning after he put the phone down. 'That was Jessica, she wants to talk to someone. I said I'll go around tonight.' Vivien had said sarcastically, 'Brian to the rescue, *again.*' He'd got back into bed, put his arms around her and said, 'She's just lonely.' Vivien had scoffed at that idea then, but now, noticing the younger woman's unsettling and erratic manner, she thinks better of it.

Jessica and Vivien stand and look at one another. Neither of them speak. Then Vivien gives a friendly sigh and says, 'Well . . .' and makes to go. Jessica suddenly says, 'I was looking for some new clothes – I have to look good – I've got a date!'

'Ah!' says Vivien and she nods knowingly.

Saying it aloud, Jessica finds the phrase is once again charged with all the triumph and excitement of earlier. Vivien responds as if to a ten-year-old. She makes her eyes big and her gestures expansive, and says, 'Who's the lucky boy then?'

Jessica doesn't seem to hear this and says instead, 'Will you come with me – there's this dress I'm undecided about?'

Vivien is flattered to feel that Jessica trusts her. She decides that maybe Brian is right; maybe Jessica just needs a little friendship. 'Okay,' she says, 'I'd love to. Just lead the way.'

As they walk Vivien tells Jessica about her first date. 'I wasn't more than fourteen, but I was dressed to the nines – mini skirt, the lot. I had on these hold-up stockings and as soon as I saw him I just ran to him and guess what? The stockings fell down. I didn't even notice! He took one look and said, "Those are funny looking socks".' Jessica doesn't laugh, but merely says 'That's not going to happen to me,' then gives Vivien an unnerving sidelong look.

They enter the shop which is called 'What She Wants' and Jessica heads straight for the dress she's tried on earlier. She moves as if hypnotized between the rails of polyester and lycra and Vivien follows contemplating the ironies of the shop's name and its contents.

Vivien is imagining a sphinx guarding the doorway stopping all who dare to approach with a 'What do you want?' She thinks that if the woman is able to condense all her desires and her needs to a simple request for some cheap slinky garment then she might gain entry. Vivien can't quite see herself passing such a test, but then she thinks, Who would want to?

Jessica scoops up the snakeskin dress and disappears behind a curtained-off cubicle. Once inside she quickly undresses; throws her jeans and sweater to the floor with distaste. Then, delicately with the fingers of a lover, she takes the dress from its hanger and slides the zip down. She steps daintily into the clinging folds, reaches behind and pulls up the zip, which makes a satisfying sound, half hiss, half purr.

Turning her eyes to the mirror, Jessica wonders how she could have been so uncertain about this dress before. She balances on tiptoes and turns sideways, sucking in her tummy, sways her hips seductively and twists her fingers through her hair. Then she leans forward, pressing her chest against the glass admiring the satisfactory swell of cleavage, and smiles a satyr's smile. Finally, with eyes closed, she kisses a cold, flat, imaginary Brian open-mouthed.

Vivien watches Jessica's feet beneath the curtain, sees the little dancing movements, the pirouettes, imagines the playful vanity.

'Have you got it on yet?'

Vivien's voice seems very near. Jessica opens her eyes and glares at the sound. Childishly, she pulls a face and waggles her head, flaps her mouth open and shut in a dumb parody of Vivien.

'Come on. Let's see. Jessica?'

She takes a final look at herself, then draws back the curtain with a flourish. She steps out, twirls and cavorts, 'What do you think?'

Vivien smiles her approval.

Jessica sees Vivien reflected just behind her in the big mirror. Vivien's wearing a winter coat and thick tights and big boots, her nose is red at the end and her eyes are pink rimmed and shiny with tears. Jessica imagines Brian having to choose between the two of them. Which will it be? Vivien in her old grannie's coat or Jessica in this beautiful dress and her high strappy sandals?

'So what do you think?'

'It looks really good. I hope he's worth it.'

Jessica smiles, lowers her head and as she passes into the changing room she whispers, 'You should know.'

Vivien says brightly, 'Pardon?' but Jessica has already pulled the curtain across.

Poor Jessica, thinks Vivien.

Poor Vivien, thinks Jessica, as she knows how bad a broken heart can feel.

Jessica stands before the mirror again, the long emerald-green curtain swaying like a forest behind her. She will buy the dress. It was made for her. She moistens her upper lip in that habitual way of hers, flicking her tongue neatly out and back again. Then she smooths her hair, narrows her yellow-green eyes and curls her narrow mouth in the barest suggestion of a smile.

ORDINARY ALICE

~

Anna Hinds

Alice is ordinary. Mixed education, bland job, many men but few interests, a broken heart, cheap lager tears, laddered tights and bleary-eyed work.

Ordinary computer stares back at *Ordinary Alice*; she reflects that she should stick to her affair with this piece of useless equipment rather than any other. ('Any other' does not use the phone, apparently.) Alice is commitmentless and her computer screen weeps dust, sympathetically. Letters appear beneath Alice's fingers, littering the screen, and she is reduced to her thoughtless, memoryless mind. Alice is reduced to ordinary efforts to work out a meal from leftover curry and baked beans (one tin). Computer is no help.

Alice defies nature and resolves to ignore all useless creatures, including this one. The computer stops being motherly and turns nasty, threatening to terminate. Alice rocks on her chair, uneasily. Alice decides to fetch next door's cat for dinner. She stops rocking and clutches the mouse, working feverishly to keep her mind off it (the cat). (Alice finds it hard to stretch to not-thinking about anything else. Especially useless machinery.) Strains of strangled cats, barmen, disappearing telephone tones, and a computer chair breaking beneath her, screech through Alice's head.

Ordinary Alice wonders if she deserved such an ordinary job. But then again, no one has ever thought highly of her. All the more reason to eat someone else's cat. The chair bends and threatens. Alice's spine cracks, low down. She is ordinary; but she can handle a chair.

Alice pretends. She dyes her hair, once a week, and does thirty sit-ups a day to keep her pierced stomach flat. She shouts at the empty walls of her flat, flirts with the fridge, rubs up against the bedroom door, and sings to the sofa. Alice is never labelled ordinary; not ordinary. Anything but.

Not ordinary; bizarre . . . psycho . . . labelled a *Prostitute*, easy for those who achingly want her to be one, suckling cigarettes and oozing frustration. A *Drug Dealer* (by those who disapprovingly, disappointedly, declare her unfit company, who father and protect the real misses ordinary of the world), infidel, drunk, whore, eccentric, worthless and blameworthy, all of these characteristics are Alice's projected Aliceness. Not ordinary. Anything but.

Alice is walking home. Stripping her soul to the bones, grinding the street to deathly dust beneath her boots, smoothing a strand of hair between her fingers. The man who sees her mistakes her wistfulness for something else, he sees *Easy Alice*, glares at her lips (red) and wishes for them. Wants to be free, wants a part of something he can get, wonders if he has enough cash on him. Alice is blissfully ignorant, lips still, eyes almost closed, the sun her only lover. She doesn't need the man, but he thinks she does. He is pleased to be able to offer money to someone in need, and if he gets a little service in return, that's great.

Alice is shocked, still, but it's happened before. Offer considered and rejected. She feels as though she has done it, as though the mere suggestion turned her into someone else. She looks in the mirror at home, not understanding; takes her lips off, ladders her tights and climbs into full-length nightie, cossetting teddy beneath a white duvet. She can't eat. The thoughts in her head make food repulsive, sickeningly sensual.

Alice drifts off into a dream.

The next day she is confident. She puts it away with *Other Blanked Incidents,* and turns into whoever she wants to be. She becomes a *New Alice*: slimlined, bashlessly tall, aloof, alone above the ground, dripping glamour. Sweating sex and bleeding dreams. Pain is nothing but a little grain of sand beneath her skin. It makes the blood scream through her veins, but increased heartbeat is good for the soul. She is refreshingly energised.

Computer is obedient, she flexes her muscles, turns down the boss's offer for lunch, fights a keyboard duel and wins. Eyeliner sobs from her eyelashes, wetting the mouse. Tears of . . . what? . . . she is crying back into ordináriness. Soon Alice will disappear, shrivelling into a pair of legs and arms in pants and shirt, silkenly clinging to an insecure body. She grips the mouse pad and calls to the computer for help, pulling herself into the screen, becoming a *Hardworking Alice*.

– It's your fault, your fault, your fault. All your fault . . . you've cocked everything up . . . look at you . . . what did you give her? Tell me the truth. You're lucky I'm a good guy.

The Good Guy watches Alice, a heroin-chic beauty tonight, with smeared tides of make-up across her cheekbones. He hands his hips, hardens his face, scowls. He hears his girl jibbering from the bathroom. He sees the culprit. A drug-stained, guilt-free specimen; he's heard of her type. Alice is silent. Wipes her hands on her trousers, holds her head straight, tries to keep her eyes from falling into dazedness. Shock is like an injection, and she is immune. She doesn't weep; her cheeks are dry as she rubs soap into them, brushes her teeth dryly, climbs in between starched sheets again. She didn't give anyone drugs, not a tablet had passed her lips.

Labelling Alice again. Snagging someone he thought was responsible, responsible Alice. Unordinary, *Irresponsible Alice*. She sighs in her sleep, folds her body inwards and drifts away dreamlessly.

She is an ordinary, ignorant mechanism. Alice wakes up. Alice walks to work in the fresh stale air, rubbing cigarette smell from her face, placing one foot in front of the other. Alice's hands do Alice's work, baby-pushing hands working the computer, the software, the hardware, not touching her eyes which beg to sleep.

That night Alice is delirious. Fever is strangling her nervous system; films play on her retina. Scripts scroll across her walls, unheeded scripts. She wants to tear them up. Alice's life wasn't a script; Alice was unordinary after all. Flames devour her arms when she reaches away from the blankets. Flames ravish the scripts, licking the edges, squeezing the life out of words. Words on the scripts are tortured and eaten; childhood words disappear, words of hope disappear, her dreams disappear. Alice is in a bombsite and all of her history past and present is eaten in the explosion. Her head rocks from side to side, mentally dodging the flames, which tongue and tease her in her bed. Alice hurls the sheet off her, but the flames are after only her flesh. The flames have burnt to ash all of the scripts on the walls and they inch towards her eyes, twisting and flickering, biting the empty air. She is afraid but she won't let them in. They start to laugh, loud, raucous laughter of those who know things . . . shrieks and gasps of hysteria, pointing sharpened fingers in the air above Alice, surrounding her neck, running down her body: look at this, they hiss. Look at this ordinary, ordinary, tattered thing. They touch fleetingly every crevice of her skin, running red-hot lines up and down. They laugh and laugh until sparkling tears litter the floor. Alice's walls are burnt and she is covered in ash. The flames giggle and smirk, dancing around Alice in big circles, skimming the ceiling. Alice's head swells blood-month like, a cocoon, she feels it blowing up. She is knocked backwards, and sleep rushes upon her. She sleeps a sleep of peace.

When Alice wakes up her mind is empty. She is free of bonds, free from the script, free of labels, people who disapprove, eyeful strangers, knowing relatives. She is freed of them in one fell swoop, or one fire. She stretches her body out as she gets up, irons out the creases, smiles at her fat toes, and tells her hair to be beautiful. In command, suddenly, at once, she leaves the house to find solitude in the bar that she once applied lipstick in. She straps herself into new heels and a *New Alice*. She pulls up her new tights and a new decision to be uncaring. She twists her hair into knots, piles on fresh eyeliner and a new toughness. She will be who she wants to be. Other people can discover in their own time.

She reaches the bar, pirouetting in chocolate velvet, slaps a forceful hand on the beer tap and scratches a red nail. *Ordinary Alice* is not ordinary. She slurps the top off her martini and leans against the bar. What does that man think, that she's *Easy Alice*? She winks lusciously through jammed eyelashes. She can chop and change italics as it suits her. What does the landlady think, that just because her nail varnish is flaky she's running on veins full of H? That because her bellybutton is sparkling with every movement, she's a wicked *Drunk Alice*? Alice shortens, her shoulders slackening against the bar. She's a nobody without their assumptions. A *Nothing At All Alice,* never changing; perhaps their labels make her Alice. What is the *Real Alice*? Is that projected too?

– *Alright love, you selling?* he murmurs as their thighs brush.

Her painted doe-eyes say no; he gestures towards the fruit machine. Alice slithers towards it a second later, uncertain and confused, drawing sharp breath.

   – *You buying or selling, honey?* He seems sympathetic; he thinks she's done too much already. *Buying Alice* or *Selling Alice*?

He thinks a free one seems in order, to get the relationship started. Usually wins people round, bit of trust.

He holds out a clenched hand and releases something into her own.

Alice turns blue eyes on the floor.

Pleased disapproving eyes all around on Alice.

Boy expects it.

They expect it.

Can't let them all down.

HAPPY ENDINGS

~

Nia Williams

What do you do when you get home, after a hard day's
work? Listen to some music? Read a book, watch the telly?
Old films – that's what I like. Weepies, comedies, musicals
– anything in black and white. I buy them on video; they sell
at knock-down prices on the high street. *Bringing up Baby.*
Laura. The Little Foxes. Anything like that. I draw the curtains,
put the answerphone on and I'm away for a couple of hours,
absorbed in pretend lives, happy in the knowledge that
everything will culminate in a swell of music, a passionate
clinch and a cast list. All the loose ends tied into a neat little
bow.

Endings. That's what we're all after, isn't it? Something
we can see, complete, done and dusted. That's what my
clients are looking for, if you want my professional opinion.

Marjorie Mills, for one. A great one for knitting. I don't
mean babies' booties or Christmas sweaters and scarves. She
used to knit people. I kid you not. Her house was crammed
from wall to wall with knitted characters: old ladies with
knitted buns and knitted spectacles; schoolboys with knitted
caps and knitted dirty knees; young girls with blue woollen
eyes and pink woollen fingernails and cleavages. Standing
in the hallway, sitting on the sofa, leaning against the fridge,
two, three, four feet high. Marjorie would go home after a
long shift on the tills, get out her needles and make herself
another friend. When the milkman raised the alarm last June,
and the police broke in through the back door, it took them

an hour to find her, lying among that crowd of chunky woollen lodgers.

A case in point, you see. Marjorie Mills was driven by the urge to create whole people, from beginning to end, knit one pearl one, row upon row, until the final loop, stitch and bite of thread. Then she'd start all over again. So much more satisfying than a *real* family, she told me. With *real* children, you don't get to see it all through.

Well, I'm the same. I like to round things off. I'm well aware that it's a sign of insecurity, a futile attempt to take control of the uncontrollable. I think we all know that, really, don't we? We all know how precarious life is. How a twitch of nature can make a mockery of our nice, safe routines. Planes fall from the sky. People who have driven the same route twice a day for 25 years suddenly forget how to do it and crash. Houses that have sheltered generations and provided landmarks for hundreds of years crumble into dust at the mildest tremor of earth. But still we go on booking flights, laying down carpets: building our rickety rafts and walkways, calling them civilizations, tottering over the abyss and remembering not to look down.

Iestyn Parry was a sales rep. Notching up 4,000 miles a year, cruising up the M4 with his cases full of party games and puzzles. One Thursday afternoon, halfway to Reading, he was listening to Radio 2 and a voice said: 'What in God's name are you doing?' Iestyn thought someone had left the wrong mike on by mistake. He sniggered. 'Look at yourself!' said the voice, and it was strangely familiar. 'Look at yourself, tucked into a gap in the traffic, hurtling along at 90 miles an hour, sticking to your place like a suicidal sequence dancer. One wrong move, one moment of impulse and you'll be smeared all over that tarmac, you and a dozen other lunatics!'

Christ, thought Iestyn, looking around him at the other

drivers picking their noses and ears. Christ, he thought, that's right. His hands tightened on the wheel. He was thinking hard, now, about controlling his car, maintaining its position, not going any faster or slower than the drivers ahead and behind. The effort made his arms tremble. He managed to pull over on to the hard shoulder and call the AA. He never drove again.

'It was as if I'd come to my senses,' said Iestyn, in our first session. 'I suddenly realised that everyone on that road was mad.' And of course, he was right. People *have* to shed their sanity, you see, if they decide to survive. They *need* to invent silly rules, of faith and gravity and stability, just to keep their footing on those rafts and walkways. Only, sometimes, people like Iestyn forget the rules. They lose their balance. A few of them – not many – reject the rules deliberately: they dive into the gulf. And what do you get then? You get chaos, that's what. Far better to cling to that raft and pretend we're in charge.

So I'm not averse to a pleasant evening's escapism. Happy endings may be a lie, but who the hell wants to face up to the truth?

Ellis Roberts reckoned he'd killed his wife. He wasn't certain, but the notion had hung around him, in the folds of his dull brown clothes, for five years. His problem was the uncertainty. Whether or not he *had* done the deed, he said, he needed to clear the matter up. Incidentally, he was a great believer in capital punishment. Definitely a man in search of endings.

Well, he hadn't killed her, as it turned out. She'd jumped off St David's Head – travelled there specifically to do it, left a note. There was no room for doubt. Ellis was at his office, filling out time sheets, when she took her stroll along the clifftop and carried on into mid-air. According to her letter, she and Ellis had been no more than polite acquaintances for many a year, and she was bored out of her mind.

So Mrs Roberts ended it all, and Ellis took it up instead, stooped under the weight of it for five years and eventually came to see me. He sat with his legs crossed, prim fingers intertwined and braced around his knee. He said:

'I'd just like to know where I stand. Did I kill her or not? I've carried it with me, this . . . possibility, for so long, that even strangers have started to notice it. They cross the road, instinctively. They don't sit next to me on trains.'

He was plagued by dreams: dreams full of intent, of malice aforethought, of vivid anger and violence. They had started when Mrs Roberts was still alive. Oh, yes, he said reasonably, he knew they were only in the mind. He knew they were inaccurate, that he had never been an angry or a violent man. But he did wonder whether they might have seeped across the pillows, somehow, and into his wife's head, mingling with her own fantasies, giving her ideas. He worried that he hadn't been upset enough when it happened.

'It's not that I don't feel it,' he said. 'But it's more like indigestion than grief. Inescapable. Uncomfortable. Bearable.'

I wasn't the first person Ellis had tried. He'd been to more conventional practitioners, who'd encouraged him to explore his feelings and talk about them, or not talk about them, if he didn't fancy it. He'd been nodded at by solemn, fastidious men who said, 'So. What you're saying is, you may have caused your wife to behave as she did . . .'

'Well,' said Ellis, in his measured way. 'Well, I could have sat in front of a mirror and done that for free. I wanted a cure, not a bloody echo.'

Of course he did. That's what we all want: cures. Conclusions. No good trying to fob off someone like Ellis with talk of acceptance or coming to terms.

'I'm not paying good money for them to tell me I've got to live with it,' he said. 'What I want is not *questions*. It's answers I want.'

Ellis, I said, you've come to the right place.

I'm not supposed to have favourites. I try to keep my relationships with clients appropriately distant. But I have to admit, I did take to Ellis. Nothing sexual – I don't mean that. God, no. I mean, I'm not saying the man was repulsive – not by any means. He had kind, hazel eyes, a rather feminine mouth, a beautiful, low baritone voice. But he didn't exactly make the most of himself. I've mentioned the clothes, I think. Drab is the word that springs to mind. Fawn-and-mustard tank tops. Biscuit-coloured trousers. He slicked his hair back – oiled it flat – and thin wedges of it would detach themselves and droop greasily over his forehead. No, I could never be accused of thinking naughty thoughts about Ellis.

But I did like him. He was different from my other clients. More clued-up. Seemed to know what was going on, right from the start.

After six sessions Ellis was prepared to concede that yes, his wife had walked off St David's Head of her own volition and no, he was not entirely to blame. But by that time he had signed up for the full course, and he was happy enough to continue. In any case, as he pointed out, there were the dreams. They hadn't stopped.

'The way I see it,' he said, absently examining a yellow wine-gum, 'I haven't yet brought matters to a head.'

He was a devil for those wine-gums. Brought a bag to every session; between us we generally polished off the lot.

It was around this time that Iestyn Parry took a walk across the M4 wielding a placard that said 'You Are All Maniacs! Get Off The Road!' I read about it in the *Echo*, and I must say

I was taken aback. For one thing, Iestyn was booked in for another three consultations, and he hadn't paid the bill. Worse than that, though, was the awful suspicion that I had misread him hopelessly. I mean, I don't take on the unpredictable or the desperate. There are plenty of other places where they can get help. Iestyn's little performance was a shock: it quite undermined my confidence for a while.

Oddly enough it was Ellis who restored it. I had decided to go back over a few basics, make absolutely sure that I hadn't suffered the same lapse of judgement with him. So I abandoned the usual protocol and asked him, straight out: 'Have you ever considered following the late Mrs Roberts's example?'

His eyes met mine in a steady, ruminative gaze. He passed me the wine-gums. He said, 'I don't like heights.'

Enough said. Everything clicked back into place. Iestyn Parry had been a one-off, an unfortunate aberration. The great majority of my clients were, as I had deduced, precisely the kind of people who would *not* do as Mrs Roberts had done. Let's face it – how many of us would? Even at our bleakest moments, how many of us would, having reached that last lip of solid turf, pace forward instead of pulling back, let the world evaporate beneath our stride? How many of us could add that extra touch of pressure, sending blade through skin and vein? Or force down the fistful of pills that would tear our guts apart? I know *I* couldn't. And neither could Ellis. I was reassured that I provide a worthwhile service. I fulfil a need.

We relaxed the rules for his final session. I brought a bottle of wine; he prepared cheesy snacks and swiss rolls. I wouldn't want this to be common knowledge, but I even waived part of his fee. I had the impression that he had gained from our meetings. It was hard to tell – such an impassive face – but I guessed that he was more at ease.

We discussed films. He liked the old war movies, which wasn't quite what I'd had in mind. In the end we settled on *Pimpernel Smith*, as a compromise. I took the video round to his house the following weekend, and we thoroughly enjoyed it. We even replayed a couple of scenes.

I'm watching the last scene now, in fact, for the third time, but without the sound. Tranquil moments like this – chewing on my wine-gum, listening to the nocturnal grunts and sighs of the house – are the most rewarding part of my job. One case completed: another about to begin. When the video's over I'll go upstairs and check on Ellis. Maybe I'll sit with him for a while. It's not usual, but as I say, he's special. In the normal course of events I do the necessary as swiftly and cleanly as possible, and then I'm off. Techniques have improved beyond recognition in the last few years: no tracks to cover at all, these days – next best thing to nature. Just as well, too. It saves any protracted investigations or doubts. And that would rather defeat the object. The aim of the game is closure, after all.

EATING FOR TWO

~

Penny Simpson

Everybody up at Wentloog knew that Erin Flaherty was eating for two. Common knowledge, it was, ever since her daughter had died.

Newspapers said the teenager had been 'incinerated' in a fire that had broken out, after a chip pan had been left unattended in her caravan. Ciara had been squatting up by the riding school for months, but Erin hadn't known about that, nobody had told her. She had made a pilgrimage there after the funeral, trying to imagine her daughter reduced to a curl of black cinders on top of scorched grass.

Hope in the Valley, that's what the pound-proud called the riding school. Welsh cobs and Shetland ponies grazing in the paddocks, like those sold in Wentloog's horse fairs in the old days. The fairs had lasted for weeks at a time, the diddies as fast with their talk as they were with their feet in the step dances. Ciara running through them all, so excited at being catapulted out of the ordinary run of things.

'Play us a giddy, Ciara, lovely.'

She had begun to play her granddaddy's fiddle when his fingers had seized up like old conkers with the arthritis. Her fingers as swift as the river where Erin rinsed out the day's washing.

'That's beautiful, that is. Really beautiful, my muddy diamond.'

Erin so proud as she listened in to her daughter playing, sitting on the caravan's steps, shelling peas into a tin bucket.

She was her 'clever curiosity' all right. Everything silent now, mind. Except for the noise of her solitary eating. Erin ate comfort foods, which she stole from discount stores in the High Street, but heaven knew, there was very little comfort to be got from the slices of processed cheese, the packets of Love Hearts, the doughnuts and the chocolate coated pretzels, which she ate by the dozen. Ate anything, see, that came in a plastic wrap, or a polystyrene box, but never food caught from the fields. Not anymore. The food she grazed on was not red in tooth or claw, but bleached out of all recognition and taste.

She had quickly fixed herself a routine. Erin ate illicit contraband stored in the pockets of her coats, then she moved on to the town's fast food joints and snaffled remnants from the diners' plates. The police told her that this had been Ciara's ploy to stave off starvation in the last months of her life. Erin imagined her daughter's pizzicato fingers scooping up leftovers, like she did the notes of a jig, swift and sure, before the store workers intervened and chased her out of their premises.

They never chased Erin away for she had grown boulder-large since her daughter's death. She was as big as a house, although she had never lived in one. Ciara's choice of last resting place made her wonder whether in fact her daughter might have been planning to come home, after all? Her social worker had found her a place in a hostel when she walked out of Wentloog. A proper place, mind. Clean pair of sheets once a week and coffee and tea-making facilities in every room. She had stayed for the one night and then turned invisible. A will o' the wisp, eating fragments left untouched on real people's plates.

But Erin, boulder-large, remained all too clearly visible to the authorities. There was no side-stepping her magnificent hips. She used them to push aside the incredulous officials and the stubborn swing doors in the stucco corridors of the town hall. She stalked those corridors of impotence, shouting out her dead daughter's name, just in case they might have forgotten her after all this time: Ciara Flaherty. Snatched up in a ring of flame. Now, her mother burnt with her public grief. As she walked, she unwrapped sweets from their wrappers. Pieces of silver foil scattered over her bulbous figure, like a conjuror's pretend snow.

'Somebody must have been up there and seen how she was living?'

'She was sixteen when she moved into the caravan, Mrs Flaherty. Ciara was old enough to make her own way in life.'

Erin tipped a packet of sherbet down her throat and its sweetness seemed to poison her. Children's treats for the mad cow mother. That's what the official was really thinking. Good as said it with her next remark:

'Maybe you should ask yourself why she left the family home in the first place, before marching in here and accusing us of neglect and suchlike!'

Fear catching in her throat now.

Ciara had left home the night her granddaddy's fiddle had been stolen. Townies had raided the caravan site, fuelled on alcopops and prejudice. Drove round in their turbo-engined cars, even killed one of the Flaherty's dogs under their spinning wheels. Blood was up on both sides of the divide. The horse dealers quick on the draw. Kitchen knives and horse whips deftly handed over under cover of washing drying out on the clothes lines, which threaded up each mobile home.

Ciara crying, huddled under the bunk bed where she slept with her two older sisters. The three of them usually folded up together like the stripes on her favourite jersey. Erin's man swearing and throwing out his punches; she, already mixing the egg whites to seal cut knuckles and lips. Her man bloody as a squashed rosehip when he fell back through the door.

'Will you just look at me, woman! Stigmata it is for *their* crimes.'

Ciara hopping to his knee. Bird-child. Face just the two eyes, the colour of granite. Eyes that cut worse than a speaking tongue.

'I'm gone from here, Mam. They think we is pigs.'

'But we knows who we are, lovely.'

'I'm gone to Johno's.'

Johno. Thick with the property-developer thieves, who had plans for the riding school site. Seduced Ciara all right with talk of champagne baths, tennis ball-sized chocolates and sex in beds stuffed full of peacock feathers, and other such nonsense. Gone, and so suddenly. Bird-child grown into girl-woman. Fifteen, just. Thin and fragile, like the horses Johno had let her ride. Erin's man had tried dragging her back by force, but her new friends had set about him with a pitchfork and a dressage whip. More cuts to mend with broken eggs.

Then granddaddy dead with the shock of the townies night time raid. Erin's man arrested and sent to prison for catching one of their number a blow to the head. Put him in a coma; cut his life's thread, like it were no more than a spider's web ripped on an open door hinge. The townie threw the first punch, she said, but the policeman's eyes were Ciara's granite-coloured eyes. Erin had been afraid to say anything more in his defence.

She only started speaking up for herself after Ciara had died, her unanswered questions lying as heavy as the folds of her new fleshy curves. She was a vast sea anemone, bloated by the ocean of lies she sucked up and then washed down with fizzy pop and sweet milkshakes. Garish coloured foods and drinks. Neither fish nor fowl. Erin had forgotten the taste of a poached rabbit, cooked fresh from the snare, flavoured with hedge herbs. Months floating in an ocean of 'E' additives and extraneous fat. Hooks and eyes on her old-fashioned, concertina corset crawling over her white sausage flesh, like dozens of little beetles. Eating for two, she was.

People averted their eyes when they saw her in the High Street. Embarrassment most like, she had thought. Recognised her, see, from the first anniversary picture carried in the *Echo*. She had been holding a photograph of Ciara, all lopsided teeth and black-tangle hair. They would glance at her and then look away again, fast. Except for Connor O'Leary, that is. One of the old horse dealers from Wentloog fair days. Saw her by chance one day in McDonalds eating her way through six cheeseburgers and three portions of fries. She had been wearing her plastic mac, the one covered with roses the size of dinner plates.

Said to her: 'Excuse me, but I'll be plucking you's later.'

Her jaws had stopped their near-constant motion. Mouth and belly so full of chewed-up food, there was no room to even draw a breath at such a blatant come-on. Connor O'Leary, sure enough. A bantam in checked flat cap and quilted body warmer. Erin blushed as red as the roses on her mac, which she had stolen from off the back of a buggy in Mothercare. That had not been right at all, to steal off a mother, even though she was all eaten up with her rage. As Connor made himself comfortable on the green plastic seat in front of her, a new feeling began to squeeze its way in under the mac's taut seams. He removed his cap and revealed hair that was as red as her blush.

'Erin Flaherty, so it is. But do you remember me?'

The fairs in Wentloog. She remembered them and, of course, she remembered Connor. He had traded his horses from a roundabout close to the caravan site, logs tethered to their fetlocks to keep them from wandering. Erin told him she was tethered to her grief. Connor O'Leary had neatly snapped her bindings with his snaggle-toothed charm. Appraised her pounds of flesh too with a horseman's practised eye. Liked what he saw, evidently. The way the roses settled like exotic butterflies on her gargantuan bust and belly. Connor looked at her like a man did a woman, even though she was long past fifty, with cushions of fat shoehorned into her silly plastic mac. Erin had blushed again and tugged at the too-tight coat, trying to smooth down her unruly folds.

Connor ignored her awkwardness. He walked her back to her caravan, his cap set back from his ginger mane, his body warmer unzipped. Erin saw how his belly curved out over his belt buckle, like a sheet caught in a gale. He saw where her eyes were wandering all right and laughed. Said he was not afraid of the sins of the flesh.

'A great idea that, Erin. Flesh is a sin and what a sin!'

He said he would share the secret with her, and, just for the once, he was as good as his word. Moulded her curves into something defiant and lovely with his twisting, slapping flipper-hands. Skins worn and torn, but precious all the same as tongue and finger slipped together in strange harmonies. Grief had not eaten her away entirely, but given her a monstrous beauty of her very own, one that he rode, like a wave.

'Erin, you're a pillow-of-a-woman, not a sharp edge to be found,' he said admiringly. 'You're nearly there, lovely. Let yourself go now.'

And let go she did, at last. Erin came, a tremendous, shuddering earthquake that toppled Connor from his bulky perch on to the floor below.

'Whoops a daisy!' he said.

He was lying spreadeagled on top of her rose-pocked mac.

Erin looked down on him from her rocking bunk bed and laughed out loud. Two years of suppressed laughter had finally been excavated and illuminated by this man's hungry touch.

'Listen to yourself, Erin Flaherty! It's the sound of bloody music.'

Fiddle gone. Daughter done. But laughter was still there, filling up the cavernous emptiness. A laughter that was as jaunty as a red plastic rose and as proud as a horseman, who had had his pound of flesh multiplied beyond the limits of reason. Erin's hunger was sated. Her lips were bruised. Her exhausted flesh a big, lovely sin, wrapped round her in a cashmere-soft embrace.

She was going to eat for herself alone from now on.

LADY MACBETH

~

Christine Hirst

Where there is fear, there is power.

Oh why, Mother, why? Thirty years of misery. Think back. Remember.

I see you now, feel your rough hands on my shoulders shaking me, your eyes full of hate look into mine, and then you let me go with the same self-pitying refrain, 'You wicked, wicked girl, what did I do to deserve you?' And up goes the apron to wipe your eyes. I stand there at seven, nine, fifteen, miserable and silent. My head down. Each year I seem to shrink. I cannot answer back. I am a bad lot and there it is. Tom smiles at Mair, as I run off to bed. The sacrificial slaughter. Those biscuits missing from the tin, I haven't eaten them; the dirty footprints on the step, they don't belong to me. Oh why, Mother? Why?

Down the street Gillie grows granite hard, facing her father and his friend, and Bethan's twin rides at her with his bike and knocks her down. This can't go on. The three of us, at breaking point, meet at school and make a solemn pledge. Things will change. Bethan, Gillie and me, inseparable. After school, we three join hands, gaze out to sea and watch the waves carry your names, and our ill wishing with them.

'Blunt not the heart, enrage it. Let grief convert to anger,' Gillie cries, arms outstretched. She and I are studying *Macbeth* for our exams. Gillie knows huge chunks by heart. Bethan is a year younger. We have written in the sand, with a crooked stick, two names each. Bethan, her foster mother, and then with tears in her eyes, her twin. She loves him, but he has suddenly, violently, turned against her. She has been fostered for her own safety. Or so they say.

'It's himself he hates,' Gillie tells her gently. 'You are part of him, that's all.'

We stare out to sea. The tide is turning, and we are turning with it.

'Who will you name, Gillie?' I ask, postponing the moment of my own awful choice. In a voice sharp as broken glass she tells us her two names, her father and his friend. We dare not ask her why, but we can guess. Poor stoic Gillie. We are silent for a long time. Then I choose Tom and add, stomach churning, you, Mother.

Gillie, very serious looks up, and after a while says, 'You know, anybody knowing they are ill wished, will bring misfortune on themselves.'

We wait. Then she adds, 'Sow the seed, and people become irrational and afraid. Where there's fear there's power.'

Bethan stares at her, then she turns and throws a stone out to sea. Gillie, urgent, says, 'Take Macbeth, once his future was foretold he killed his greatest friend because he was a threat.'

The very worst kind of betrayal. She has us now. I break the silence.

'The ancient Celts believed,' I say in a whisper, 'that the spirit of the person is contained in their hair.' Nervous, I go on, 'And, if you wrap a piece inside a written curse . . .' I cough, stop, adding all in a rush, 'then pass it over the flame of a lighted candle three times, in a circle, it will come true.'

Bethan gasps, open mouthed, excited, frightened. We look at Gillie. She has a new authority about her. Her eyes hold us.

'The thing is, they have to know.'

I think of you, Mother, and I know she's right. Your malice haunts me. I am never free. Gillie watches the gently lapping waves. 'Choose a name,' she says. She looks at me.

I cannot speak. 'Shall we have your Mother first?' she offers, like a gift.

'She never wanted you,' Bethan reminds me gently. She knows, from her real Mam, what you did to me, before I saw the light of day. But it is too big a step. I can't begin with you, even after all you did. You are too strong.

'Choose Tom,' I say suddenly. 'Tom is cruel. Take away the only thing he cares about. Drop him from the football team.'

Gillie is jubilant. She thinks the choice both simple and inspired.

'That's settled. Now let's decide who will do what. Bethan?'

Eager to begin, Bethan turns to me, 'I'll do the thing with candles, if you will get some hair.'

I nod.

'Menna,' says Gillie, looking straight at me. 'Get inside his head. Scare him. The next match will see him out.' Then she smiles, hugs us both and says, ' Let's join hands.'

We move around in a circle, very slowly, Gillie singing, 'When shall we three meet again. In thunder, lightning or in rain?'

I sing too, a bit off key, 'When the hurly-burlys done, When the battle's lost and won.' Then all at the same time, we say 'Here after the match!'

'We are turning wicked,' Bethan says, laughing.

Gillie opens her arms wide to the sky and shouts, 'Our great revenge will cure this grief.'

Now three strands weave together to form a stronger thread, Bethan, Gillie and I. That day I learn to grow. Then the wicked women kiss each other on the cheek and come as close to vanishing as they can. I run home, stronger, happier.

Home. I turn my key in the lock, open the door and go into the back room. There I see your china dog smashed and scattered on the hearth. Tom is standing over it. He does not speak. The front door slams. You are there, standing in the doorway, staring.

'Menna did it.' It's Tom, playing the old, old game. And you, on cue, join in.

'You wicked, wicked girl.' Your eyes blaze and then the old refrain. 'What have I done to . . .?'

This time I cut you short.

'It's what you failed to do, get rid of me. Don't think that I don't know.'

Fear flashes in your eyes, and for a moment the balance shifts. The battle lines are drawn. Power and fear. Fear and power. You slap my face so hard I fall against a chair. As I look up, Tom is laughing. I turn my head and look into your eyes.

Then as now. Stone. Stone. Thirty years the same.

I square up and take my time. You hardly know me. 'Wicked is as wicked does,' I say, very calm, and very still, and then I add a quiet threat, 'You'll see.' I glance at Tom, and walk out of the door to my room. I am in the process of becoming something other.

Later you all go to bed and after a while, as if in a dream, I find myself cutting a piece off Tom's hair as he lies asleep. In my room my fingers touch it lightly. There is an innocence in its softness and its shine. For a moment I glimpse another happier life. Not steeped in wickedness like mine. My heart sickens with a longing for the thing I need most. Loving arms to hold me. Yours, Mother. But you have pushed me down into the dark. I wrap the curl in tissue and put it out of sight.

That night I dream I see you standing in the doorway. You fill my room with such an air of evil I shrivel up to nothing. Then I wake, cold with sweat. It is dawn, the birds are singing, there is no one at my door.

I run along the streets to meet Bethan at the school gate.

She takes the tissue carefully and slips it in her bag. She bites her lip, her eyes are full. She is about to tell me something when we hear someone call our names. It is Gillie. She rides up on her bike, her face alive with bruises, but she smiles.

'We're in luck, full moon tonight.' We look at her. 'To strengthen our resolve,' she whispers and then takes her bike over to the sheds.

'*Macbeth* again?' asks Bethan. I'm not sure. But it will help me anyway. Bethan has other things to worry her. She tells me, through her tears, that her twin is now at special school. They say his need is greatest and so he must be the one to live at home.

'Mam chose him instead of me.' Her voice is hoarse with pain.

I hug her and say, 'We'll sort it out, you'll see.'

We behave quite normally at school. I work hard now. I win approval. I have hope. Gillie works harder. She is driven. She wants to go away to Drama School. She needs to get a scholarship to pay her fees. She works as if her life depends on it.

At home things change. Each night I flash Tom a look of such dislike he is disturbed. The match draws near. The night before there is talk of nothing else. Tom, so proud, so full of hope. If there is a penalty will he take it? The odds are that he will. I seize my chance.

'If you miss,' I say, 'It will make you angry with yourself, fit to foul someone.'

He hears, but does not to reply.

'Yes, anger works against you,' Mair says. She plays hockey for the school. Now she plays into my hands. They talk to you and to each other, not to me. But I have sown the seed. Now, I simply have to wait and tend it, make it grow.

That night, under the full moon, I feel my way along the

landing to Tom's room. My heart thumps. I am afraid of the sound of my own breath. I pass your doorway, Mother, and all the hurts of childhood scream in my ears. They strengthen me, and urge me on. At his door, I pause, nervous as a spider. Then I open it. I stand quite still.

'Tom,' I whisper, 'What I said at tea time you will do.' He starts to toss and turn. His eyes stay closed. I stare at him. Macbeth hath murdered sleep and so have I. Then I close his door and creep downstairs, as far away from him as possible. In the back room his football kit is all laid out, like offerings at a shrine. I grab his shorts and back in my room I stuff them underneath my bed, right at the back. I have done everything I can.

The next morning Tom is pale. He says he is not sleeping well. He looks at me confused, then looks away. I smile, but not at him, and leave early.

The match is after school. Tom has to play in borrowed shorts, too big at the waist. I notice how he fidgets. Gillie, Bethan and I stand together. We play another match within the one we see. You stand with Mair, Mother, well away from us. The struggle starts. It's you and me. When he plays well you win, I lose. Then Gillie starts to fret. But just before the end something goes amiss. Tom takes a penalty and it is caught. He turns red with shame, then white with rage. The ball moves the wrong way. So, as the final whistle blows he runs at the captain of the other side, and with a vicious tackle from behind, he brings him down. The lad screams out in pain. A crowd gathers. A broken leg they say. Tom walks off in shame. He knows he will not play again.

The wicked women fly to the beach. Gillie on her bike ahead, Bethan with her hand in mine. We are shining with success. We laugh and laugh, going over it, talking all at once.

Gillie takes my hand. 'Macduff is on the move,' she says. 'The beginning of the end.'

We find the crooked stick and write the names again. Next to Tom the simple words, Done For, like an epitaph. We talk of you, Mother, shunned at the shops, a bully for a son. And Tom friendless, a failure, all alone. I start to think I have some special gift.

Gillie thinks this too. What I was becoming, I've become.

Bethan asks if we can help her next and we agree. We will meet again, on the beach, after school tomorrow. A wind springs up ruffling the waves out at sea. The sun goes behind a cloud, turning the air colder. It is time to go. Gillie waves and rides away. I walk back with Bethan who, full of magic, tells me that her Scottish aunt wove a curse into a sweater for her husband, so he would drown at sea.

'Did he?' I ask, and she laughs, nodding her head as she waves good bye.

I walk up the path to our front door and turn the key. The house is cold and empty. No one comes home. In my room I work until it is dark. There are sounds about the house now, but no one comes to me. Something is wrong.

The next day, at school, the Headmaster sends for me. I knock on his door and wait. My heart pounds in my head. He calls me in and tells me to sit down. He looks at me and then he says, 'Menna, your brother Tom is seriously distressed. Your Mother wishes me to speak to you. She says you undermine Tom all the time at home, and then disturb his sleep.' He leans across his desk looking straight at me. 'Is this true?'

I cannot speak. I should have known. I am no match for you.

He leans back, his eyes dark with dislike. 'Yesterday, during the match, she says you distracted Tom before he took the penalty. Do you deny it?'

There is nothing I can say. Tom caught my eye, and you caught mine, Mother.

'That is serious, Menna. He is a promising young player, with a very bright future.'

'How is the boy whose leg he broke?' I answer back. I answer back at you.

'Bruised that's all.' The air turns black.

'So Tom will play again?'

He nods. And then he open his drawer and shows me a pair of shorts, the ones I stole.

'Under your bed, Menna. A petty, spiteful act. Your Mother gave them to me. Explain this, now.'

My tongue is in a trap. I cannot speak. I fall and fall, lower and lower still.

'Menna,' he says, 'your Mother called on Mrs Jones who cares for Bethan. They found these.' A candle and some hair. A scrap of paper charred around the edge. I take the paper from his hand and read the words, 'Get Tom out of the team for Menna's sake.'

I am unmade. I lie like bits of shell, wave-smashed on the shore.

'Menna, I will not have this. You will report each day to the office and work there until you have taken your exams. You will not speak to any other pupil. I am sending you home today. Please wait outside.'

As I leave the room he picks up the phone. I wait outside, pinched with fear. Then you arrive to take me home. I want you to forgive me, to take my hand. I look at you. I cannot speak. You look at me without a word. I watch your mouth curl in contempt. Then you turn your back and walk towards the door. I follow you in silence.

The days pass veiled, grey. The moon is black, malign, Mother. Your moon. I spend my time with shadows.

On my sixteenth birthday in July, I am sent, with all my things, to your sister, Anne.

When the results are due at school, my uncle goes instead of me. Ten straight A's. The Headmaster says that I could flourish in a different soil. He suggests another school and university. Anne and my uncle ask me what I think. They will pay. They have grown to like me and are kind. I am the child they never had. I cry and cry and then I say, 'Yes, yes, please.' And so my new life starts and I do well, but you are always with me, Mother, in my head.

Bethan, at her own request, goes to Scotland to her aunt. She is happy there. Gillie gets into Drama School and soon becomes well-known. Glorious Gillie free at last. Once I go to see her in *Macbeth*, Bethan comes down too. We have supper together after the play. It is like old times, the three of us, together, happy. We raise our glasses. We have come through.

But Tom. Tom is . . .

What? What is Tom, Mother, ruled by the bottle, a hopeless drunk?

Now you lie before me, old age has got you by the throat, depriving you of speech. I stare into your eyes. You turn away. I do not speak with any sound but you hear me. You hear the unborn child, the girl, the woman, three voices all in one.

Your eyes turn back to me. I search them carefully for just a glimmer of affection. I give you this big chance.

Stone, stone. Time changes nothing. We live in circles, and I am back where I began. Round and round, yesterday, tomorrow and today. The same old fight. I look at you once more then look away, and switch my bleeper on. It goes off straight away, I am needed on Ward Eight. Needed, Mother, me.

I have to move quickly. I take down the card above your bed and add 'Nil by Mouth'. I change your doctor's name to mine, and then I hook it up again. Your eyes are closed.

You will not look at me. 'Sister,' I say, as she appears, 'Ten thirty in the theatre. I'll do this one myself.'

She smiles at me impressed, and strokes your arm.

'Who's the lucky one?' I hear her cheery voice, as I run past the other beds. 'That Doctor has a special gift, they say.'

CHARMED LIFE

~

Lindsay Ashford

'How could you?' I whispered. 'How could you kiss something so . . . disgusting?'

Mimoza and I were lying belly down in the meadow, the grass squeezing its juices into our clothes. But as I wavered, she was mesmerizing her conquest with her treacle-toffee eyes. Eyes that never flickered as her mouth slid into a dangerous smile.

'We're just a middling kind of people,' she whispered back. 'Not perfect like Gorgios.'

The word 'perfect' shot from her mouth like spittle and I blushed to the roots of my hair. What I had said was stupid. It was the kind of thing my mother would have said.

I reached out again to stroke his skin. It felt smooth and cool, like stones in a river. I let my finger trace the curve of his spine and closed my eyes. Tom Evans. I must think of Tom Evans. I squeezed my eyelids until the image in front of me began to blur.

I had practised kissing a lot that summer. Usually I had to make do with an apple, but tomatoes were better. Their skin was the right colour for a mouth and the name reminded me of him.

But this was for real. I was about to kiss a living, breathing mouth. I bent my head and puckered my lips. But at the last moment I opened my eyes. It was no good. I drew back, squinting in the sunlight.

'I'm sorry,' I hissed. 'I want to do it but I can't.'

As I watched Mimoza rhythmically stroking hers, my own little fellow slipped away into the long, soft grass.

'Never mind,' she said, seeing without looking. 'You can have mine.'

She told me I must keep him in my bedroom for a week. I wondered how I would hide him from Mother. 'Stroke him every day and talk to him if you really want to charm him,' Mimoza said. 'Romany, mind, not Welsh; his kind won't listen to nothing but Romany.'

This struck me as rather peculiar, but almost everything I had done that summer with Mimoza was strange. Strange but exciting. Like picking snails off trees and walls and watching her boil and then fry them in butter and herbs. To eat.

Mother would have had a fit.

'Mimoza,' I said, 'Can he really grant my heart's desire?'

'Yes.' She looked at me with knowing eyes. 'As long as you don't go wishing harm on no one. What you send out comes back on you seven-fold, see.'

'What about Tom Evans? Will it work on him?'

She raised herself up on her elbows and I could see the deep cleft where her tawny skin disappeared beneath her dress. She was much skinnier than me but she had breasts. I wanted breasts almost as badly as I wanted Tom Evans.

'Course it'll work,' she said. 'Long as no one else has got to him first.' She pulled up a daisy and started plucking at its petals. 'God is good and the Devil is not so bad to those whom he likes,' she murmured, tossing the flower over her shoulder.

'What did you say?'

'Oh nothing,' she replied, looking away. 'Just thinking about the wedding, that's all.'

I kept my secret for three whole days. Whenever Mother was out of the house I would get him from under the bed. I did exactly as Mimoza had said, stroking him gently and repeating the half-dozen Romany words she had taught me.

'A toad, is it?' My father had managed to get from his bedroom to mine.

'Oh!' I cupped my hands in a vain attempt to hide the little creature.

'Don't worry,' he smiled, 'I won't tell her.' He walked unsteadily into the room. 'You going to show me then?' Gasping with effort he sank down on to my bed.

I held out my hand and watched as Da and the toad eyed each other.

'Funny how people always think of them as slimy,' he said. 'But their skin's as dry as yours and mine.' I watched him finger the lump on the side of his neck. Touching it had become an unconscious habit for him. Today it looked even bigger. Mother said it was mumps, but when I had them I'd had swellings on both sides.

'Does your Mother know about the gypsy girl?'

I started. How did he know about Mimoza?

'I've seen her waiting for you by the gate to the woods.' He chuckled. 'I might be an old wreck but these still work.' He pointed to his eyes.

'What do you think I've been doing stuck in that bedroom all week? It's amazing what you can pick up just looking out of the window.'

'You won't tell her, will you, Da?'

'No, *cariad*.' He turned his head away and drew his lips into a tight circle. 'How long is your friend staying?'

'She doesn't really know. Only a few weeks. She's to be married at the end of August.'

'Married? She doesn't look any older than you.'

'She's two years older. It's just that she's very small and dainty – not a bit like me.' I sighed and looked down at my big hands clutching the tiny toad. If Mother knew what I had been touching she would make me scrub them. Scrub them over and over again until they bled.

'And who is it she's marrying?' he asked, wincing as he raised himself off the bed.

'Her cousin. She doesn't like him all that much, I don't think. But it's their tradition. She said they always marry within the family to keep the Romany blood pure.'

He reached for the window ledge, almost losing his balance.

'Da . . . can I ask you something?'

He turned and looked at me. 'Depends what it is,' he said, smiling.

'Do you ever get lonely sleeping on your own?'

'Well,' he sighed, staring out of the window. 'I'm a bad sleeper these days, Molly. I toss and turn a lot in the night.'

I went over to him, cupping my hands together to prevent the toad escaping through the window. 'So you don't mind then?'

I minded. I minded because of Mimoza. She said husbands and wives only slept apart if they had fallen out of love.

I could remember the day it started. The day she made him move into the spare room. He had taken me fishing and I had caught my first trout. Mother walked into the kitchen as he was showing me how to gut it. She just stood there staring at the fish blood on his fingers.

I pushed the image away with my usual trick of thinking about Tom. Every girl in the village fancied him. I smiled to myself. If I was married to Tom I would never want him sleeping in any other bed but mine . . .

'Watch it, Molly, she's coming,' Da said, pretending not to

have heard my question. I glanced out of the window. Mother
was striding up the path. There was someone with her. It was
the doctor.

'Da,' I said, 'You only saw him yesterday.'

'I know, *bach.*' The corners of his mouth turned up, but I
could tell from his eyes that it wasn't a real smile. I should
have realised there and then how ill he was. But I was too
busy worrying about love.

'He's probably brought those new pills he promised me,'
Da went on. 'Now you hide that little chap away and go out
and get some fresh air, eh?'

Mimoza was waiting for me by the gate.

'How's the toad?' she called, as we raced through the
woods.

'My Da knows,' I panted, as we reached the clearing where
the caravans stood. 'But he's promised not to tell.'

We flopped down on the grass and watched the dogs and
the small, naked children scampering about in the sunshine.

'Mimoza,' I shaded my eyes as I turned to look at her.
'They must have loved each other once, mustn't they?'

She shot me a puzzled glance. 'Who must?'

'My parents. They must have been in love in the beginning
or they wouldn't have got married.'

Mimoza shrugged, saying nothing.

'I'm sure I can remember her kissing him once.' I rolled
on to my back and closed my eyes. 'It was Christmas time.
I can't have been more than about six because we still had
the King. They were listening to his speech on the wireless.
When it finished she pulled a piece of mistletoe from behind
her back and kissed him right on the lips.' I rolled back and
looked at Mimoza. 'But she never does it now.'

I cocked my head on one side, waiting for her to say

something. But she was still gazing at the children and the dogs. 'He tried to kiss her on her birthday,' I went on, 'and I saw her screw up her face as if it was the most horrible thing she could imagine.'

'Like mother, like daughter,' Mimoza said slyly.

'What do you mean?'

'Just thinking about that toad,' she smiled.

'But that's different!' I raised myself on my elbows and stared at her indignantly.

'Not to your Ma, girl,' she sighed, shaking her head.

When I got back to the house I could hear voices. It was Mother and the doctor. I crept along the hall and listened at the kitchen door.

'You should have come to me sooner,' he said.

'How long?' Mother's voice sounded strange.

'A few weeks; maybe a month or two at the outside.'

'And there's nothing you can give him?'

'Apart from morphine for the pain, no. That growth on his neck is cancer. It's gone into his glands. I'm sorry, Mrs Llewellyn.'

'But he can't be dying,' she said in a hoarse whisper. 'I've kept everything so clean . . .'

I turned on my heel and belted out of the house, running blindly through the woods. Twigs scraped my face and hair and tears blurred the path but I didn't stop until I reached the clearing.

'It's my Da!' I blurted out as I burst through the door of Mimoza's warm, smoky caravan. She tried to calm me down with a cup of strong tea mixed with yellow liquid from a brown bottle. The trees looked as if they were melting and Mimoza's eyes seemed to dance before me like black dice tossed from a cup.

'I want to change the charm,' I mumbled. 'You've got to help me, Mimoza. Please say you'll help me.' I tried to fix my eyes on her slippery face. 'I don't care about Tom Evans anymore. I just want Da to get better . . .'

'You know what's wrong with your mother, don't you?' she said.

'My *mother*?'

'Yes.' Mimoza's eyebrows arched like a blackbird's wings. 'She's got the *mochadi* fever.'

'What on earth is that?'

'*Mochadi*? It's the word we use for dirty things; unclean things – you know. Cure her first if you want to cure him.'

The next morning I woke with a thumping head and lay staring at the pattern on my bedroom curtains. In the sober morning light her instructions were quite monstrous.

'You must take the toad and cut it in the neck,' she had said. 'Cut it in the same place as your father's lump. Then press the toad's wound to your father's tumour. Bind the toad to his neck like a live poultice. An outer dressing must be bound over the one holding the toad in place and this must be changed every day by your mother. No one else must touch it, only her. The toad will draw the cancer from your father's body but your mother must not remove the toad until it is dead.'

Well that's it, I thought. Da was doomed. If Mother refused even to kiss him how was she going to be persuaded to do something as gruesome as that?

I dragged myself out of bed, gingerly pulling the curtains open. There was Mimoza, waiting by the gate.

'I can't do it,' I whispered, standing by her in my night-clothes. 'I've told you what my mother's like. She'd never agree to it. Never in a million years!'

'Oh, but she will,' Mimoza smiled. 'Just fetch pen and paper and a knife and I'll tell you what to do.'

I felt like an executioner as I held the toad in my left hand and picked up the knife with my right. 'I'm sorry,' I breathed. The toad sat unblinking and I tried to convince myself that he didn't mind. That, could he speak, he would have told me he was happy to sacrifice himself to this higher purpose. Bending down I kissed him on the head.

I could smell Da before I opened the door of his room. It was a stale, musty smell, like the tea towels in the church hall that Mother said never got washed often enough. It was dark inside. The curtains were drawn. I was scared that I wouldn't be able to see what I was doing.

I crept further into the room and peered at the figure on the bed. He was so still I thought he might be dead already. In a wave of panic I rushed across to him, almost dropping the bundle in my hand. But as I reached the bed I saw his chest rise and fall.

I didn't know anything about drugs then, but Da must have been so far gone with the morphine he probably wouldn't have woken up if I'd marched into the room singing. He hardly stirred when I began to bandage his throat. By the time I had finished my clothes were sticking to my skin. I left the note on the bedside table and crept out of the house.

Mimoza and I became spies after that, climbing a tree near the house and watching what my mother did. At the end of each day I would return to my hiding place in the woods.

I lived on fried snails, porridge and a kind of black pudding made from the blood of a goose. I spent my evenings stitching beads and ribbons for Mimoza's wedding dress. The beads winked in the firelight like a toad's eyes and as I worked I wondered if Mother was really doing what my note demanded. What if Mimoza had misjudged her? What if she was glad to have me and my germs out of the house?

'Mimoza,' I said, when two weeks had passed and I was trying not to cry. 'Can you give me your word of honour that the charm will work?'

She drew in her breath and looked up at the sky. 'If you give your word to a person how can you keep it?' she said.

A tear splashed onto the wedding ribbon in my hand and Mimoza looked round sharply.

'Cheer up, girl', she said, 'She sleeps beside him every night now.'

'How do you know?'

'Oh, didn't I tell you?' She looked as if she was blushing, but she turned her face away. 'I've been going spying at night sometimes.'

It took three weeks for him to die. Mimoza came early one morning to wake me. 'Come quick!' she said.

I wept when I saw Da hobble down the path to the gate. I ran from the bushes, arms outstretched, trying not to hug him too hard. Kissing him, I realised that my lips were on the very spot where the lump had been.

'Yes, it's gone,' he whispered. 'Here's your mother coming – give her a hug too.'

It was strange. Mother held out her arms. I couldn't remember the last time I had seen her do that.

I searched for Mimoza in the woods the next day, but the clearing was deserted. No dogs, no children, no camp fires or cooking pots. The caravans had all gone. I wondered why she had left without saying goodbye.

The day after that was Sunday and I cheered up a little. On Sundays I got the chance to dress up and see Tom. But he wasn't in church. I craned my neck, searching the pews for his face but he wasn't there. None of his family had come.

When the service was over the butcher's wife made a beeline for my mother. I heard her say Tom's name and I edged closer, staring at the floor so they wouldn't notice the blush seeping into my cheeks.

'Ran off, they did,' the woman said, savouring the news like a mouthful of meat pie, 'And her a gippo! It'll never last!'

When I got back I shut myself in my bedroom and stared out of the window. There was something fluttering on the gate to the woods. A note. I knew it was from her and I didn't want to read it. But my legs took me down the stairs and into the garden as if they had a will of their own.

'I never changed that charm, Molly,' she had written in her strange, sloping hand. 'It was the love of you and your mother what healed your Da. You charmed Tom Evans right to your door but it was me he found when he got there.' And at the bottom of the paper she had scrawled: 'Don't be wishing harm on me now, girl. I just can't go kissing toads no more.'

FISH

~

Fiona Owen

In the hall stands the goldfish tank, gone all green now. The fish can just be seen, idling among the few strands of slimy reeds. Sometimes they come up to the edge of the glass and peer out, their mouths working, their gills flapping in the thick pea-soup water. Their gold is dissolving into the gluey depths of the tank, settling on the bottom like a discarded robe; in the breathless hush of water, they are preparing to die.

When Huw tells his father about the fish, his father seems not to listen. He seems not to hear. It's that woman, thinks Huw. She's brainwashing him. Each time they go to visit Mrs Jackson and Grettie, Huw sees the fish and the fish see him. Each time, they come right up to the very edge of their world and stare out through the glass at him, with round flat eyes.

'Why don't you clean out the fish?' he asks Grettie, when they're alone.

'She won't let me,' says Grettie, eyes wide towards the door. 'I think she wants them to die.'

'Why did she get them then, in the first place?'

'They were Daddy's,' says Grettie, and then her eyes fill up and overflow.

The hall is the only room in the house that hasn't got carpet. The kitchen has carpet and the toilet has carpet. This makes Huw uncomfortable. What happens if someone pees onto the floor, like his dad does sometimes, in the middle of the night, and like he himself does, often? Boys haven't got such good aim. He remembers his mother always calling him a sprinkler. 'You're as bad as your dad,' she used to say.

Huw thinks there's a smell in the toilet, beneath the floral air-freshener. It's all that sprinkled pee that's soaked into the carpet. You can't vacuum it up. He doesn't fancy the idea of having a bath at Mrs Jackson's house. He doesn't want to walk barefoot in the pee. It's bad enough wearing socks.

Mrs Jackson calls herself *house proud*. She likes Huw to take his trainers off at the front door. He has to leave them alongside his dad's boots and Grettie's shoes, all lined up underneath the fish tank, which sits on a dark old leggy table with twirling edges. Huw tries not to look at the fish tank when he's taking his trainers off, in case he meets eyes with the fish.

'Come on, Huw,' shouts his father, from inside the house.

'Yes, hurry up, Huwie,' comes Mrs Jackson's voice, thick like golden syrup. 'We're all waiting to eat.'

Huw has a knot in one of his laces. The harder he pulls at it, the tighter it gets. He knows without looking up that the fish are lined along the glass, all three of them, mouthing at him in soft liquid voices, whispers that wake Huw from sleep or pierce through his dreams.

'I can't undo my lace, Dad,' he shouts, too loudly. He can hear himself breathing quickly and has a vision of himself in a relay race at school when he was younger, trying to catch up, to catch the boy in front, feeling the blood in his ears pumping, that sense of time overtaking him.

Belinda Jackson appears in the doorway.

'Can't you, love?' she says, cooing like a pigeon. 'Here. Let me help.'

Huw doesn't look up, but struggles harder with the lace. He has a sense of bulk beside him, of soft cushioning breasts and flowery perfume. Just as her hands reach towards his, the knot comes apart between his fingers.

'Done it,' he says, a stark note of triumph in his voice. He jumps up and away from her.

'You're so independent, you are,' says Mrs Jackson. She says it in a voice like honey, but Huw can't meet the hard grey of her eyes.

The table is round, with a peach-coloured table cloth and blue patterned crockery. There is a bottle of wine on the table and wine glasses. Grettie is sitting between Mrs Jackson and Huw, her hair long and straight down her back. She eats without looking up and sometimes she rocks slightly, as she swings her legs under the table. Huw can see his father's face is flushed. That means it's almost time. Huw holds out his leg so that Grettie kicks him accidentally.

'Ow,' he says. 'Why did you do that?'

'I didn't do anything,' says Grettie, her enormous pale eyes gaping in her face.

'Huw,' says his father, warningly. Mrs Jackson is pouring him more gravy, and chuckles.

'It sounds just as it should do,' she says. 'They're starting to relax with each other, that's all.' She beams round the table. 'Pour the wine, Tom. Give the kids just a teensy-weensy bit, eh?'

'I don't want any wine,' says Grettie.

'Oh go on, just a little,' says her stepmother. 'It's a special occasion.'

'I'll have some,' says Huw, anxious not to miss the opportunity and also keen to out-do Grettie. He is thirteen, after all; she is just a kid.

'You can have some orange instead,' Huw's father says to Grettie, as he pours wine into Huw's glass. 'And half a glass will be enough for you,' he says to his son. 'And just this once.'

Mrs Jackson holds her glass up for him to fill and she smiles at him the whole time.

On their way over to see Mrs Jackson and Grettie, Huw's father had said, 'How would you fancy Grettie as a little sister?' Huw had made a noise like being sick, which was only a slight exaggeration of the way he was really feeling. He'd known it was coming; he'd read all the signs. But it still came as a jolt, like an electric shock striking him just under the ribs. 'Because I know she'd love to have you as her older brother.'

Huw could feel himself sealing shut, tight as a clam.

'I mean, poor kid. No dad . . .'

And no mum either, thought Huw, feeling an unexpected pang of compassion for her.

'Belinda does her best, of course, but it's been hard. She's looked after Grettie like she was her own daughter. I mean, how could a father just up and off and leave his own kid, eh?'

Huw suddenly wanted to ask Grettie questions, things he'd never thought of asking before, about missing fathers and wicked stepmothers. Because Huw was convinced Mrs Jackson was somehow wicked. The fish had told him. Mrs Jackson was really a witch who'd put a spell on his father.

'Dad,' he said, bursting his own silence. 'Do you *love* Mrs Jackson?'

'I wish you'd call her Aunty Belinda. Mrs Jackson is so formal.'

Huw tried it out in his head. *Aunty Belinda*. The sound made him shudder.

'Do you love her?' he repeated.

'Well, yes. Sort of.'

'Like Mummy?'

'No, not like Mummy,' said his father. His father always

talked about his dead wife in hushed church tones and his eyes would drift away from Huw to some other time.

'How then?'

'Well, she's good company. She's companionable, a good laugh. She fills a hole in my life.'

'Made by Mummy dying?'

His father said nothing for sometime and Huw thought he'd forgotten the question. Then he said, 'Nothing could fill that,' and Huw sighed deeply. He hadn't realised that he'd been holding his breath.

Huw has a ritual. Every Sunday night, he locks himself in the bathroom and drags the old wicker chair to the sink, so that he can climb up and kneel on it. Then he stares at the mirror non-stop and after about five minutes, his mother comes. His face changes ever so slightly so that it gets more oval. His curling hazel hair grows around his face and falls to his shoulders and his eyelashes grow longer and curl up more. Those are the only necessary adjustments. Then, with his mother's face smiling back at him, he whispers her his secrets, his worries, his latest fears, and she whispers back the answers in her soft wise voice. Her brown eyes brim with love for him, her only son, and her thick hair gleams under the strip-light. Before she goes, she kisses his lips a cool lingering kiss. Then she vanishes back into the mirror, leaving only her breath on the glass.

'We've got a surprise for you two,' says Belinda Jackson. 'Haven't we, Tom?'

'Well, yes we have.'

Huw picks up his wine glass and swills the wine down nervously, all in one go. Then he burps and Grettie shoots him a quick contemptuous look from beneath her eyelashes.

'Can I have some more wine?'

'No, you've already had half a glass. That's quite enough.'

'Tom, let him have a drop more. He needs something in his glass for the toast.'

Huw can feel the wine already working. His lips have turned to rubber and his lower abdomen feels soft and pulpy.

'Yes, the toast,' he says, wanting to giggle out something about marmalade.

'Oh, all right then. Just for this once.' His father pours him half a glass more.

'Your father has something to tell you, Huw,' says Mrs Jackson. 'That's what this meal is all about.'

Huw knows she wants him to look at her, to look up and smile expectantly as if keen to know the secret. But he has already guessed what's coming, so instead he stares at her breasts. They look even more enormous than usual, as if they're all squashed together and are clamouring for space. They appear over the top of her blouse in mounds and Huw has the insane impulse to lean over and bite into them as if they were ripe juicy fruit.

'Huw and Grettie,' his father says, scraping his chair back awkwardly, so that his napkin slips from his lap. 'Belinda and I have come to a decision that will affect us all.'

Huw sticks his legs out under the table, trying to catch at Grettie's swinging legs.

'What we figure is this: Belinda's on her own with Grettie and I'm on my own with you, Huw, so it makes sense to pool our resources.'

Huw has hold of one of Grettie's feet between his ankles and Grettie is going pink in the face trying to pull free.

'So we've decided to get married and then we can all live together as one family.' Huw lets go of Grettie and stares across at his father. 'Married.' It sounds like an echo. Now that the word is out and hanging suspended over the table, it seems too close, too real. Huw feels as if he's fallen into a nightmare.

'Yes, Huwie,' says Mrs Jackson. 'Isn't that wonderful?'

'No, it's not!' Huw jumps up, knocking his chair over backwards. His head has filled with a giddying red fog. 'You're a witch and you've put a spell on my dad. He doesn't love you. He only loves my mum.'

'Huw! What are you saying?' His father stands up too and comes round to Huw and takes his shoulders. 'Huw, you apologise to Belinda.'

'No, I'll never apologise to her. I'm not going to live here with a witch!' And Huw shakes himself free and runs away, up to the bathroom.

Huw is panting so that his breath mists the mirror. It is cold against his cheek, and through the glass, he can see the whole bathroom in reverse: the pink bath, the pink wash-basin set into an ivory cabinet, the rows of creams, shampoos and talcs, the wall-to-wall pink carpet, and the toilet in the corner, from where Huw can already smell the dirty yellow under-smell of urine. Huw knows he must speak to his mother, but it isn't Sunday and this isn't his house, so he's not sure the magic will work and he's not sure he should even try. But his eyes are prickling with hot ready tears and he feels that, if ever there was a time to test the magic, then this is it. He goes to the door and checks the lock just one more time. Then he goes back to the mirror. It is full length, so all he must do is stand in front of it and wait. He knows how to focus his eyes so that everything around him fades into grey background and all he can see is himself. He knows he must stare into his own brown eyes without blinking until he is squeezed to a hot pin-point shape on the glass. Then he feels himself grow loose and limp and it is at that moment that his mother steps forward, out of himself and into the glass.

'*Cariad*,' she whispers to him. Huw feels himself wrapped by cool slim arms. She kisses his forehead, his cheeks, his lips.

'How's my baby boy?'

Huw licks away his salty tears. 'I wasn't sure you'd come to me, here,' he says.

'I'll come whenever you call me,' his mother whispers, with gentle eyes resting on him.

'This is the house of a witch,' he says, wiping his nose with the back of his hand.

'I know. But you have stronger magic.'

'Dad is under her spell.'

'Yes, but you can break it.'

'How?'

His mother smiles at him through the glass, her hair the colour of autumn.

'You must rescue the fish.'

'The fish!' Huw can feel his face flush in excitement. 'They whisper to me. She wants them to die.'

'I know. They are part of the spell. If you rescue the fish and set them free, the spell will be broken and all will be clear to you.'

'Then I'll do it,' says Huw, and he places his palms against his mother's and their lips meet softly.

Just then, Grettie's voice comes through the door. 'Huw, let me in.'

His mother vanishes and Huw is left wiping the smudges hastily from the mirror.

'Who were you talking to just then?' Grettie stands in the bathroom, while Huw locks the door again.

'Nobody,' he says.

'But I heard you.' She is looking at him curiously, more openly than before.

'No you didn't,' says Huw. Then, 'What do you want?'

'They sent me up,' she says, indicating the door with her head. 'First your father was furious and wanted to come after you and make you say sorry. Then he thought he should maybe let you cool down first. Then *she* sent me up to bring you down. Really, I think she just wanted me out of the way.' She looks at Huw through long fair lashes. 'You're right, you know.'

'About what?'

'About her being a witch. I've known for ages. It's because of her that my Daddy left home one night and never came back. Now I don't know where he is.' She is looking down again, her pale hair falling across her face like a thin veil.

'I know how to break her spell,' says Huw, lowering his voice. He moves closer to Grettie, feeling suddenly protective of her, suddenly akin to her in spirit.

Grettie wipes at her face and looks up at Huw through wet eyelashes. 'How?'

'It's to do with the fish. I have to rescue them.'

'They're Daddy's fish.'

'Yes, but they're dying. If I – we – don't get them out of that tank and into fresh water, they've had it.'

'But where could we take them?'

Huw's brow crinkles in thought. 'I don't know yet. A river, maybe.'

'Or a lake,' says Grettie, her eyes widening. 'I know one.'

'Do you?' Huw takes her arm. 'Where?'

'It's in the woods, not far from here.'

'Then you must take us there. Tonight.'

'Tonight?' Grettie sounds suddenly doubtful. 'It'll be dark,' she says.

Huw waves a hand dismissively. 'There's no time to waste. Now, we must go downstairs and pretend. I'll say I'm sorry, but I'll cross my fingers, so it won't really count. Then tonight, late, I'll come for you, and we'll go to the lake.' He peers closely into Grettie's face. 'Okay?'

Grettie nods, but she is chewing at her bottom lip and her pale face looks bleached.

Huw dreams he's in a dark wood, alone. He is searching for something, but he can't quite remember what. He is walking with his arms outstretched, as if he's sleepwalking. Brambles tear at his pyjama bottoms. An owl hoots overhead. There is a rustle among the ferns: something is approaching. Huw turns to see an orange glow, like the prelude to a sunrise, and as he watches, the orange becomes golden. Soon, the light is dazzling, filling the glade where he now stands and out of this sunbeam light rides a beautiful lady with lustrous russet hair astride a gilded stallion that is somehow both a horse and a fish. Suddenly, the beautiful lady holds out her arms and Huw sees with joy that she is his mother and he opens his mouth to call to her, but instead of his own voice, another voice comes. There is a moaning low in his throat, a deep groan that builds and builds. Huw puts his hand to his mouth, forces his fist down his own throat. His mother is calling to him but the moan is louder. It's blocking out all other sound. As Huw struggles, with his hand tearing at the inside of his throat, the moan crescendos, rises in pitch, becomes a high mocking cackle . . .

Huw wakes with a jolt. He is breathing hard and his nose and mouth feels wet. He reaches to the bedside table and turns on the lamp.

'Damn,' he says. His hand is smeared with the red of blood and the pillow is stained. His nose is still bleeding, so, tipping his head back and cupping his hand underneath his nose, he slips out of bed and goes out onto the landing. The house is in darkness except for the thin light from his bedside lamp. Downstairs, the dining room clock chimes the hour of two. Huw shivers. He tip-toes across the landing, walking carefully to prevent creaks. He'll have to go to the bathroom, until his nosebleed stops. But he has to pass the room where his father is lying with the witch. The blood is dripping from his nose onto his pyjama top and it's awkward trying to step noiselessly with your head tilted back. He knows this is the dangerous part of the landing and their door is slightly ajar, too, so he must take extra care. Then, from within the witch's room, come noises: grunts and growls and breathy groans. A moaning like pain. And Huw knows it's time and, true enough, the fish begin calling to hurry, hurry, and he abandons his search for toilet tissue. As if carried along by air, he finds himself in Grettie's room and by her bed.

'Grettie,' he hisses, shaking her roughly. 'Wake up.'

Huw has prepared. He stole a plastic food bag from one of the kitchen drawers. Now it is filled with water and Grettie is standing holding it, while Huw is up on a chair, netting the fish. The hall is filled with an eerie green light, emanating from the fish tank.

'Here they are,' Huw whispers triumphantly, as he lifts the net from the tank. He climbs down from the chair and they both gaze into the net at the fish, who lie placidly among the sludge scraped up with them. Even in the dim green light, the fish look tarnished and ill.

'It's almost as if they know we're helping them,' whispers Grettie.

'Of course they know,' says Huw, carefully releasing the fish into the plastic bag. 'Not long now,' he tells them. 'Soon you'll be free.'

The night is black and still, and Huw is wishing he'd brought a torch. He has his anorak on over his pyjamas and although it's mild, he feels on the brink of shivering.

'How much longer?' he says.

'Just up here,' says Grettie. She is walking ahead slightly, with quick small steps, and Huw is suddenly struck by her whiteness, by the way she seems to glow in the dark. Her cream-coloured hair spreads around her shoulders, and her face, pasty at all other times, now gleams as if lit from within. Even the length of white nightie that hangs beneath her jumper seems to be giving out light. Now she stops by a wooden stile set into the fence.

'This is it,' she says, and her eyes fill her face like moons.

Huw has tied the plastic bag at the top and carries it in front of him in case the brambles tear it.

'Where's the lake?' he says.

'It's in the middle of the wood. It's quite easy to find once we get on to the main track.'

The path they are following is narrow and uneven and the trees seem to close in behind them. Grettie glides ahead, lighting the way for Huw, who stumbles along, catching his feet in tufts and trailing vegetation. The trees clutch at him as he walks, stroking his hair and patting his shoulders. And all the time, he carries the fish ahead of him, as if presenting them as a gift.

Suddenly the path opens out into a clearing. Either Huw's eyes have adjusted to the dark or it has got lighter, for he can see more easily around him. They are standing in a glade which is encircled by trees and undergrowth.

'Where are we?' he says.

Grettie is walking the circle, lighting the air as she goes. Then she stops and cocks her head to one side, like a dog listening.

'Grettie,' says Huw, uncertainly. 'What are you doing?'

'We're near,' says Grettie. 'I'm just finding the direction.'

Huw looks about him. This clearing is like a cul-de-sac. He can't see another way out. He turns back up the path they came down. There might be a path leading off it that they missed. It's dark, without Grettie, and the brambles seem worse. He holds the plastic bag higher. But his foot hits against something and he goes sprawling down among the vegetation. He can think of nothing other than the pain, as the nettles and brambles close around him, stinging and striking at his hands and face like a hundred vipers. There is a moment of blackness, of silence. Then he remembers.

'Oh God,' he whimpers, and struggles upright. 'The fish.'

The thorns tear at his clothes as he feels his way forward. It's so dark. It's as if the trees have grown in minutes to shut out the night sky.

'Grettie,' he moans. Then louder, 'Grettie. I've lost the fish.'

She appears at his side like a candle.

'I fell and I've lost the fish,' says Huw, crawling up the path on his hands and knees. 'They could be anywhere.'

Grettie is behind him, rummaging. He can hear her rustling in the bushes. Then she says, 'Here they are!' and Huw clambers unsteadily to his feet. Holding the bag up, they can both make out that it's spurting water like a watering can. Huw tries to cover the holes with his hands, but it is useless. He gives out a howl of frustration that stirs the trees like a breeze. Then Grettie says, 'Follow me.'

They head back down the path into the clearing. Huw cups the bag in his hands, feeling the water leak out like blood. Grettie floats across the clearing and slips behind a tree and Huw follows, close behind. A narrow rabbit track leads them round a thicket and down an avenue of closely growing evergreens. Then, without warning, the trees seem to side step, and there in front of them is the lake.

They both kneel down at the water's edge. The lake is like a black mirror, stretching out into the darkness. Huw struggles with the knotted bag. The water's all run out and the plastic has closed around the fish like cling-film. He rips the bag open and they peer in.

'Are they alive?' whispers Grettie. As if in reply, they see the faintest of wriggles: the flutter of a tail, the flap of a gill.

'Good luck,' Huw says to them, and then tips the bag inside out, so they fall with a plop into the lake. For a minute, they float on the surface and Huw thinks he's killed them. Then there is the kick of a tail, the flash of old-gold and, one by one, the fish swim away, down into the depths of the lake.

Huw leans over as far as he can and stares into the water after them. As the ripples subside and the surface of the lake smoothes over to its mirror finish, a face seems to compose itself upon the water. The detail is missing, but Huw recognises the smile. He lowers his face closer to the surface of the water, and whispers, 'Have we done it? Have we broken the spell?'

The face smiles back at him tenderly, then seems to dissolve, leaving him staring into his own reflection.

'Huw,' says Grettie, and her face glides into view like a swan. 'Will everything be alright, now?'

Huw pushes himself to his feet and wipes under his nose with his forefinger. He feels like crying. But also, he feels grown up: wise and responsible.

'Maybe. Yes.'

Grettie is gazing up at him and shifting from one foot to another, pointing her toes like a ballet dancer.

'You should see yourself,' she says. 'All blood-stained.'

'I had a nosebleed,' says Huw. 'I forgot.'

His eyes wander across the lake's smooth surface. Detail is appearing out of the grey dawn light. All around them, the birds have started up a rowdy chorus.

'Might as well go home, then,' says Grettie, attempting a pirouette.

'Okay,' Huw says, turning for the trees. 'Might as well.'

GUILTY

~

Siân James

My mother had a great-aunt Hester. Hetty. She was born back in the nineteenth century, had died before I was born, but of all my relatives, she's the one I'd liked to have known. Hetty.

Her mother had died in childbirth and she was brought up, rather grudgingly it seemed, by her grandmother. Life was hard for elderly widows in those days, and Hetty was allowed a small share in her grandmother's poverty. The cottage was small and sparcely furnished, food, mostly bread and potatoes, was always in short supply and to make matters worse, she had no other children to play with; the nearest house being two miles away. She went to school in the nearest village, three miles away, until she was eleven, though her grandmother would keep her home whenever it suited her. In spite of her erratic attendance, she learnt to read and write; indeed when my mother was clearing out her house, forty years later, she came across three or four books she'd had as school prizes.

The headmaster's wife, a Mrs Matthews, had a large family and would often call her in to give her parcels of out-grown clothes and a slice of bread to eat on the long walk home, but, as she told my mother on one occasion, had never invited her in to play with her own children. I suppose no one took much notice of her.

It was her love of wild animals and her ability to rescue and tame them which gave her life a purpose. It was con-sidered a fairly easy task to rescue a fledgling magpie and keep it as a pet until the following spring when it flew away to find a mate, but even her headmaster was impressed when a blackbird accompanied her to school one year, waiting in a tree outside until the end of the day. 'Sir, Hetty's taught the blackbird to whistle Bobby Shaftoe,' one of the big boys announced. And Mr Matthews listened to their duet, Hetty inside the classroom, the blackbird outside, and afterwards patted her on the head. One spring, she rescued and reared a baby squirrel, a red squirrel, far more wild and shy than the grey, and even after she'd released it back into the woods, it would appear on a branch from time to time when she walked to school, as though still acknowledging a distant kinship. 'I've got a dratted flea in my bed,' her grandmother complained around this time. 'Oh, but I mustn't tell you or you'll be wanting it for a pet.'

In spite of her limited diet, Hetty grew very tall, so that when she had to leave school to nurse her grandmother who had developed sciatica and could do nothing for herself, she was able to get a morning job at Bryn Teg, the nearest farm, with a Mrs Delia Evans who'd been given to understand that she was thirteen, and who was to prove a good friend.

Hetty's grandmother died when Hetty was fifteen and at that point Mrs Evans suggested that she should take a full-time, living-in job at the farm. She was about to move in when her father turned up. He'd disappeared when his wife died, probably unwilling to contribute anything to his child's upkeep, escaping to South Wales where he'd got a job in the mines and re-married. His second wife had eventually thrown him out because of his habitual heavy drinking and occasional violence, so that he'd returned to his native village and hearing of his mother-in-law's death, had gone along to her cottage, hoping for temporary accommodation.

He was astonished to discover his daughter there; he'd hardly given her a thought for fifteen years. (By this time he'd had two daughters by his second wife, but was equally indifferent to them.)

Hetty listened to all his troubles, accepted his presence as she'd accepted every other of life's burdens, made up her grandmother's bed and prepared to look after him. He was by this time a sick man.

She cared for him for twenty years. He had a miner's disease, dust on the lungs, which prevented him from working, but not from drinking; he could manage to cajole money from her even when she had barely enough for food. My mother once asked her whether she'd been able to feel any affection for her father. 'No, only sorrow,' she'd answered tearfully. He died in 1914, just before the beginning of the first world war.

The war caused few changes in Hetty's life; she didn't miss any luxury food items because she'd never had any and having no sweetheart or brother, wasn't heartbroken about the young men who were being sent to France; she cared and worried about them, hated the idea of war, but wasn't personally involved.

She wasn't again invited to live in at the farm; by this time Mrs Evans had five children so there wasn't even an attic available, so she lived alone in her isolated cottage, becoming more and more of a recluse. She worked at the farm as the indoor maid-of-all-work, lighting the range at seven every morning and scrubbing out the dairy and the flagstone floors of the kitchen and back-kitchen and the long passages, washing and mangling all the 'rough', the bed linen, the towels, the overalls and aprons, cleaning vegetables, making bread, churning butter. Mrs Evans didn't ask her to work outside because she knew how upset she got at the way the farm animals were treated; she'd always send her home early when Emlyn Gelly arrived to kill the pig; she didn't even ask her to pluck a chicken or skin a rabbit. What she was able to do, she did with all her strength, but there were things she wasn't able to do and Mrs Evans accepted that. 'She's not like other people,' she'd say, 'and perhaps that's not such a bad thing.' She was aware that Hetty went round the rabbit snares that her husband laid out around his hedges, but never let on; she herself had often been sickened to see the poor mutilated creatures. 'Shoot them, by all means,' she used to tell her husband, 'I know what damage they do, but it can't be right to torture them.'

'I saw you out in Top Meadow earlier on,' she once said when Hetty had arrived a few minutes late for work. 'Was it mushrooms you were after?'

Hetty had blushed to the roots of her reddish hair, but had scorned to tell a lie. 'No, not mushrooms. Too early for mushrooms, Mrs Ifans. But when I find some I'll bring them up for your breakfast, be sure of that.'

'I know what you're doing Hetty,' Delia Evans said after a moment or two, 'and I don't blame you. You've got a soft heart, that's your trouble, but I won't say a word.'

What else did she find to do with her time after her long day at the farm? She occasionally went to evening service at Bethesda chapel on a Sunday when the weather was fine, but Mrs Evans told my mother that she wasn't a great one for God. 'I don't understand what He's doing, Mrs Ifans, letting all our young men face such danger. Ifor Stanley has been killed, they say, and his mother a widow with only him to help her with her bit of a smallholding. And even if those Germans lads are wicked as Mr Isaacs, Bethesda, seems to think, they've still got mothers, haven't they?'

'It's not for us to reckon it out, Hetty. But thank goodness my boys are too young to go to the Front. They took Mat Brynhir, as it is, and two of our horses.'

It was in the spring of 1918, the morning of Palm Sunday, when Hetty found the injured man in the woods. She was picking primroses and violets to put on her grandmother's grave and they were so scarce that year that she'd had to go deep into Arwel woods before she'd got enough for a decent bunch. The man pulled himself up to a sitting position and stared at her. 'Don't split on me,' he said. Hetty didn't understand much English, but she understood the pleading in his eyes. She put down her flowers and took off her shawl and put it round his shoulders because he'd begun to shiver and sweat. 'I'm on the run,' he said. 'On the run from the army. They'll shoot me if they find me. Don't let them know.'

'No,' Hetty said. 'No, no, no. I get you food.'

She looked hard at him. She had sometimes seen animals being driven to the slaughterhouse in town. It was Palm Sunday. She gathered up her flowers and walked quickly back to the cottage.

There was some soup on the hob. She heated it up, put some into a covered pot, placed it, with a piece of bread and a spoon, into a basket, put a blanket on top and walked back into the wood, walked hurriedly, fearing that the man might already be dead: she knew starvation when she saw it, knew the smell of death, too.

He hadn't moved; had either been too weak, or had perhaps trusted her. 'I'm a deserter,' he said – she didn't know that word – 'and they'll shoot me if they find me.'

'No,' she said. 'I say no.'

Then she started giving him spoonfuls of soup, very small amounts at first.

'Good,' he said.

'Cawl,' she said.

'Cawl,' he said.

She went on feeding him until his eyes closed. Then she

took the shawl she'd lain on him earlier and folded it for a pillow, laid the blanket over him, and told him, as well as she could, that she'd be back when it was dark. She wondered whether he'd be still alive and wondered what she'd do with him if he was. However would she get him back to the cottage? He was certainly too weak to walk. Perhaps she'd have to leave him in the woods until he got stronger.

She still had some of her father's clothes which she'd washed and ironed but hadn't managed to give away because no tramps, these days, seemed to come so far out of their way as her cottage. She'd burn his army uniform and give him clean clothes and he could hide away in her grandmother's bedroom until the war was over.

After her dinner, the remains of the soup, she walked the three miles to Bethesda chapel to put the bunch of flowers on her grandmother's grave. She didn't intend to stay for evening service, but went into the chapel and for once managed to pray, tears falling down her cheeks as she did so. 'Let him live. Let him live.'

The Reverend Isaacs came in as she was coming out. 'Are you all right?' he asked.

'I'm all right. But what about the soldiers at the Front?'

'God cares for them, Hetty, every one.'

'No He doesn't,' Hetty snapped back at him. The Reverend Isaacs was to report that at her trial.

As soon as it was dark, Hetty set off to the woods with a basin of bread and milk in her basket. She shivered a little, remembering the story of little Red Riding Hood which Miss Jenkins had read to them in the Infants', but then smiled at her fear; she wasn't a pretty little child but a grown woman, nearly forty years old, her hair already grey and her back already stooped. And the poor soldier she was hurrying to see was weak as a sickly lamb.

He was still alive. She got him up to a sitting position and fed him the bread and milk.

'Good,' he said.

'Bara llath,' she said.

He looked worse than any tramp, he hadn't shaved for weeks, he stank of urine and faeces, but Hetty was ready to risk everything for him. He was a frightened man on the run and she had to hide him. She had no option.

He wasn't ready to try to walk, whimpering when she tried to get him to his feet, so, reluctantly, she had to leave him where he was for another night.

The next morning she was up before dawn' to take him some gruel before going to work. She found him a little stronger, got him on his feet, said he had to walk a short distance to a place where he'd be more adequately hidden. After walking a few steps, he collapsed onto the ground and wept. 'My feet are on fire,' he said. 'No more walking.' She undid the laces on his boots and as she tried to ease them off, was almost overpowered by the stench of his feet. He smiled at her for the first time. 'Thank you,' he said. She began to feed him the gruel, but he was able to take the spoon from her and feed himself.

She left him a bottle of tea and a piece of bread for his dinner and hurried to the farm.

'Hetty, you're not yourself this morning,' Mrs Evans said. 'Aren't you well?'

'Thinking about this war, that's all. When will it end, say? What does it say this week in Mr Ifans's paper?'

'Always telling us it's going to end, but nobody knows is my guess. And all our boys getting killed. Katie Williams, Hendre Fach, has lost three of her four sons and she won't last long, doesn't leave her bed, they say. Joe Morris's boy has been sent home but he'll never be right, his feet are like webbed feet, Joe says, something to do with being in those wet trenches for months at a time, and he may have to have one leg off because of the gangrene . . . Great Heavens, girl, sit down for a minute. Put your head between your legs, you've gone as white as milk. You'd never do as a nurse, would you? Too soft-hearted, by far.'

Hetty sat for a whole five minutes before she felt up to getting on with the butter making. And the whole time she was churning the word gangrene, gangrene, gangrene went round and round in her head.

That night she went off again with her pot of soup. 'Cawl,' he said, as she lifted the lid. 'Good cawl.' He ate heartily.

'Walk now,' she said when he had finished. She helped him to stand, hoisted his arms over one of her shoulders and half-carried, half-dragged him along the dark path. Four times, when his groaning became too much for her, she had to let him rest for five or ten minutes. The journey, less than two miles by her reckoning, took almost four hours.

She let him lie on the doorstep while she went in to light a candle and re-kindle the fire. The kitchen had an earth floor with a rag rug in front of the hearth. She dragged the rug a yard or two into the room and brought down the quilt from her bed to lay on it; she knew he'd never manage the stairs that night. When she went out to help him in, he was already asleep. She had to wake him and force him, quite roughly, to take the last few steps. He lay down with a groan and was asleep again in less than a minute. Then she banked the fire, put a china chamber-pot at his side and set out again for the wood to retrieve the blanket and the shawl.

It was after midnight when she got to bed though she had, as usual, to be up at six. Her body ached with tiredness, but she couldn't sleep. She knew she could find him food, knew she could hide him away since no one ever called on her, but what would happen if he had gangrene? At last she slept but dreamed about the war, about soldiers, Joe Morris's son amongst them, turning into large green frogs croaking in the slime of the trenches. The plague of Egypt, she was saying as she woke.

'You're looking ill again today,' Mrs Evans said. 'Sit down and have a basin of porridge before you start on the dairy. Can't have you fainting away again.'

'You're very kind to me, Mrs Ifans,' Hetty said. And burst into tears.

'Are you in trouble?' Mrs Evans asked her. But then realised that she couldn't be, she was surely too old, had never even had a sweetheart as far as she knew, she was tall as a man, her chest was flat, her hair scraped back in a bun. 'Are you unwell? Are you having heavy bleeding, something like that? It's quite usual, you know, at your age.'

'No, it's nothing like that.'

Hetty sat over her porridge, still weeping, and Mrs Evans suddenly decided that what she needed was a bottle of tonic. 'I'll send you home early this afternoon, Hetty, so that you can go up to see Sal, Penpwll. She's got all the old herbal powders and mixtures that are better than anything Dr Forest prescribes and you save a guinea as well. Sixpence is all she charges. Spring is a hard time for man and beast and as you know I've got my sister and her family coming for Easter so I'll be depending on you at the weekend.'

Hetty was pleased to have an excuse to visit old Sal, though she lived on the far side of the moor. She told her how she'd lost her appetite, how tired she was all day and how she wasn't able to sleep at night. 'Please give me the strongest tonic you've got. It was Mrs Ifans, Bryn Teg, sent me. She says you're better by far than the doctor and cheaper, too.'

'She's right, gel fach. This is my special mixture, this green one. It's bitter, mind, but it purifies the blood like nothing else. You'll be strong as a stallion when you've got this down you. A teaspoonful twice a day in half a cup of water and that will be sixpence halfpenny.'

Hetty felt buoyant as she walked home, confident that the bitter green medicine would be just the thing for her soldier.

That evening she managed to get his boots and socks off, and though his feet were sore and bleeding they didn't seem disfigured. He whimpered like a puppy as she put his feet into a bowl of warm, salt water, but seemed ready to do whatever he was asked. The next morning before she went to the farm she managed to get him upstairs and felt he was now safe. She washed him and gave him one of her father's old shirts to wear and helped him get into bed in the best room, which had once been her grandmother's. The English she'd learned at school was coming back to her and she was beginning to understand most of what he said, though she found it more difficult to talk to him.

'I'm Hetty,' she said when she came home that evening. 'You?'

'Billy. Billy Mason.'

'Mam? Dad?'

He nodded his head. 'Live in Gloucester. You have parents? Mam and Dad?'

'Dead.'

'I'm sorry.'

'You write to Mam and Dad?'

'No,' he replied in an anguished voice. 'No. They mustn't know I'm alive. No one must know.'

She picked up his uniform which was caked with mud and sweat. 'Burn,' she said. She took every piece of his clothing out into the garden, built a bonfire and stood over it until nothing remained but clean ash. She went upstairs again to try to tell him that he was no longer a soldier, but he was fast asleep. She breathed more easily.

'The tonic is doing you a lot of good, Hetty,' Mrs Evans said at the end of the week.

'Oh, it is.'

The next three weeks passed with relatively few problems. Billy, though unable to eat much, seemed a little stronger each day. He walked to the window of the bedroom and sat there for much of the time she was at work. It was a warm spring. Hetty was pleased that he didn't mention coming downstairs.

Occasionally he'd talk about the war. When he did, he'd forget that she was there, talking fast and wildly so that she wasn't able to follow much of what he said. 'Jack. My pal, Jack. Went to look for him. Nothing left. They could only bury one arm. Almost everyone killed or wounded. Bodies everywhere. Trip over bodies. Parts of bodies in the trenches. I had home leave. My parents didn't understand. I left home. Too frightened to go back to France. Too frightened. They'll shoot me when they find me. They'll find me. Soon. Soon.'

On those evenings when he became hysterical with fear, she'd put her arms round him and rock him to sleep.

It was midsummer when he started raving and shouting uncontrollably and Hetty realised that he had a high fever. She didn't know what to do with him, then. He'd take no food or water. Hetty didn't go to work, but all she could do was wet his lips and put a cold flannel on his forehead and tell him over and over again that he was safe.

One evening, when she hadn't turned up at the farm for three days, Mrs Evans called on her. Hetty let her in and took her upstairs. 'He's dead,' she said in a very calm voice. 'I tried to look after him but he died. He was a soldier. I found him in the woods. Billy Mason from Gloucester.'

She couldn't remember much of what happened after that. Mrs Evans was very kind and stayed with her while all the others came and went; Mr Evans, the doctor, the policeman, the undertaker who took away the body. 'I promised they wouldn't find him, but he's safe from them now,' she said over and over again. While Mrs Evans spent her time telling them all that Hetty was different from other people, too soft-hearted, but a good woman for all that.

They didn't listen to her. She was put on trial for harbouring a deserted soldier and was throughout the subject of great ribaldry. 'That's one way of catching a man.' 'Aye. She burnt all his clothes and wouldn't let him out of bed for three months.' 'An old maid's revenge. I reckon he'd have been better off in France.'

She was found guilty and sentenced to eighteen months hard labour, but was released a month after the armistice when she'd served only six.

During her trial, which had been widely reported, her two half-sisters from South Wales – one of them, my great-grand-mother – contacted her, visited her in Swansea Jail and remained in touch with her ever afterwards. 'Two sisters I never knew I had,' she told Mrs Evans. 'And so kind, you wouldn't believe.'

In the spring of 1919, she was considered strong enough to go back to work at the farm.

Later that year, Billy Mason's parents sent her a letter of thanks and a framed photograph of their son, taken when he had first joined up. He looked so young and unmarked by war that she didn't recognise him. All the same, she kept it on the dresser for the rest of her life.

I have it now on my mantelpiece. 'Billy Mason from Gloucester,' I tell friends. 'No, not a relative. Just a soldier my great-aunt Hester picked up in the woods.'

MERMAID

~

Jenny Sullivan

'*Daddeee*. Play with me, please Dad?'

'Why don't you make a sandcastle, sweetheart.' The man brushed a fly from his chest, his eyes closed against the sun. 'Daddy's got a bone in his leg.'

'Everyone's got bones, Daddy. You're silly.' The voice turned petulant. 'You never play with me any more.'

He opened his eyes, squinting, and rose from his spread towel, brushing sand from his shins. 'What shall we do? Play ball?'

The child shook her head. 'We left the ball behind.'

'Well then, what?'

'Make something.'

'A sandcastle?' He stooped, lifting the garish bucket, reaching for the plastic spade.

'No. Something else. Sandcastles are boring.'

'If you say so, sweetheart. A boat? A shark? A mermaid?'

'A mermaid. A beautiful mermaid, please.'

The woman did not raise her eyes from her novel, gave no intimation that she had heard the conversation. A slight breeze fluttered the pages and she trapped and held them, the fingers already holding a cigarette.

Man and child selected a flat area of damp sand and he measured it with his eye, gauging width and length, and with a small stick, began to draw an outline.

He sent the child to collect shells, weed, and other treasures discarded by the tide, and from time to time as he worked he raised his head to follow the small, industrious shape silhouetted against the sheen of sand.

He dug, shaped, smoothed, patted, and gradually the mermaid grew beneath his hands. First the rough outline and then detail: the small oval face, blank-eyed, the uneven flow of sand-hair. Rounded shoulders below a slim neck, arms stretched out, one raised, one lowered, as if she struggled to backstroke free from the sand. Small, high breasts, the lightly barred rib-cage hollowing to a perfect indentation of navel on the curved belly.

He frowned, assessing his work. Stooping, he etched more deeply the hollow of an eye-socket, changed the curving smile a little, pared width from the chin, just as the child arrived with her trophies. Spraddle-legged, she considered.

'She looks a bit like Mummy.'

His laugh was harsh. '*Much* too fat for Mummy, sweetheart.' He glanced sideways at the woman, unmoving except for the slow turn of a page, the continuous spiral of smoke from the chain-smoked cigarettes, silent in her canvas chair. They might have been invisible, or she deaf and blind.

Together, man and child completed the figure, heaping and patting into place the curve of tail, the sweeping flukes, and then they decorated it. Great black-green swathes of weed for hair, nacreous morsels glinting in the eye-sockets, bright pebbles ornamenting her earlobes and a modest mosaic of alabaster fragments over the high breasts. The tail was their masterpiece: dozens of glittering shards of sea-glass, mother-of-pearl, milk-blue mussel shells, and rainbow snailshells scaled from hips to flare of fluke. They worked until the afternoon grew cool and the sun reddened the sea, but at last the mermaid was finished. And still the woman turned her pages, smoked her cigarettes and did not look at man, child, or the mermaid in her own image.

They left mermaid and sea reluctantly: the child turned at the wooded entrance to the beach and looked back. The late sun glistened on the mermaid's blind eyes.

That night, only the child slept dreamlessly. The man lay awake beside his sleeping wife, listening to the pull and suck of the incoming tide, imagining it creeping, destroying, washing away the curve of cheek, the outstretched arm, the small mounded breasts and belly, obliterating the mermaid gradually and completely until there was nothing but flat, chaste sand.

The woman dreamed of the mermaid, whose creation she had watched beneath lowered lids, noting the resemblance to herself and choosing to say nothing. She, too, dreamed of the incoming sea, but when wetness touched the mermaid's outstretched fingers, she saw them flex and move, and as the water rose the mermaid that wore her face swam free, rolling in the pull of the waves, sluicing sand from a gleaming body, twisting and writhing until she was completely free of the clutching sands. An iridescent tail flickered, lambent drops cascading, and the woman smiled in her sleep and stretched, knowing the freedom of the open seas.

THE PALACE OF ANXIETIES

~

Christine Harrison

'You don't mind heights then,' they had said when she moved house after her husband had died. The house itself looked as if it might one day take a run and jump over the cliff into the sea. It was called 'The Sea-Gulls'.

Sometimes when looking out of the window, she was overcome with vertigo. She felt she might fall through the glass. It was a horrible feeling – she would see the doctor about it.

Opposite the bay window, on the wall, was a large framed photograph of the Dean in his vestments. He was looking out to sea. On the sideboard underneath this picture was a bowl of artificial fruit, hard shiny apples, strawberries – an orange too, especially hard and bright as in a children's picture book.

There had been no children – the Dean had been enough trouble. 'Though he always kept on the straight and narrow,' thought the widow, 'as one would expect, of course.' Her eyes flickered over the wallpaper which she had not chosen, flickered quickly over the photograph.

She kept his warm outdoor cloak in the hall. The photograph and the cloak – that was all that was left of him. She put on her cardigan which she had knitted through the widowed winter as she had sat with that wallpaper and the new gas fire half on. It was time for her morning walk.

This was the excitement of the day. Every morning, on this walk, she got a little closer and a little closer to the cliff edge. Closer, she thought, as she walked, the pale harebell sky fitting like a dome over the bright landscape. She opened her mouth to the salty breeze. The winter was over. It had been quiet, dead, almost a hibernation. Only, emerging from it, there was this giddiness. The daisies at her feet spun round like wheels. As she turned back to the house she felt almost as if she were falling. The doctor did not seem very concerned when she told him. 'Perhaps it's time for a holiday,' he had suggested. She thought he looked as if he needed one himself.

'Would you come with me?' she had wanted to say. 'You are after all my doctor and I shall need company on this holiday and there is no one I can ask. They are all too constrained by my widowhood, you know, and being the Dean's widow doesn't help.'

This imaginary conversation continued in her head as she walked giddily back to the house. 'Of course I'll come,' said the doctor. 'Just let me get through this lot in the waiting room. They are such a nuisance. Not one of them is sick, has anything really wrong with them. Where shall we go? Not Bournemouth, that's all.'

'What about the Isle of Wight?'

'I've never been there. There are lots of cliffs I believe.'

'Yes,' she said, 'but also nice tea gardens.'

'I'll be with you in a jiffy,' said the doctor.

The widow got back to the house just in time before her dizziness nearly overcame her. She looked through the Yellow Pages for sorceress, witch, magician. She had heard about these people.

She explained about her giddiness, just talking about it made it worse, she said. 'Do you know where to find us?' asked the sorceress. She sounded very far away as if muffled inside something.

'It's where the old museum was, I believe.'

'Yes, that's right.' The voice retreated even further.

The widow picked up her tapestry handbag and her car keys and left the house. 'Strait is the gate,' she murmured to herself, 'and narrow the way.' Fragments of ecclesiastical quotations often interjected themselves into her thoughts – it was not surprising.

The car started up with a jolt. It was only a minute or two to the museum, she could have walked but was feeling too unsteady.

The tall building swayed over her. She climbed the stone spiral staircase, flight after flight. She was aware of a cold solid silence in the well of the staircase but did not look down. She knocked on a door that had been painted blue.

'I don't bite,' said the sorceress who was sitting on a battered but shapely armchair, a small table beside her. On the table, but not in the middle of it, was a vase with a single tulip, its petals beginning to curl open. The widow sat in a chair the covers of which hung in silky rags.

'This used to be the room where they had Victorian things, corsets and fans and things. Mincing machines,' said the widow, 'and mangles.'

'Things change. Life is fluid,' said the sorceress. She mixed her precious oils. 'Why do you resist it?'

She took one of the widow's hands and massaged the palm vigorously with her thumb. The widow sighed.

'Sigh away,' said the sorceress. 'It is good for the soul.' She took the widow's other hand. 'If you don't mind the use of the word.'

'My husband was the Dean,' said the Dean's widow. 'The word was on his lips every day. To me it is an everyday word.'

'How interesting,' said the sorceress. Her eyes were dark brown and shone like marbles. Her hands were a gardener's hands, the nails short and blunt. If there was a silence the widow might say to her, 'Do you like gardening?' and that would fill the awkward gap. Perhaps the tulip came from the sorceress' garden.

'Do you like gardening?' said the widow presently.

'My clients are my garden. Their problems are the weeds,' was the reply.

There was another silence.

'Is a cheque alright?' asked the widow.

'Of course,' said the sorceress. 'If you have a card of course.'

'Come back next Tuesday morning, Emily,' she added. 'At ten o'clock.'

No one these days called the widow Emily. The name dropped in her lap like a flower or like a little present, gift wrapped.

On the way home she stopped and bought some biscuits. The Mothers Union ladies were coming to tea.

They were waiting for her outside the house, wandering all over her garden. 'Come in, ladies,' she said fumbling with her key. 'You will all be blown away.'

She made the coffee and set out the cups and saucers. 'I get this ringing in my ears,' she said.

'Oh so do we, so do we,' they said. 'We think nothing of it.'

'A biscuit? Or a scone perhaps – not all that fresh.'

'How you must miss the Dean,' they said not for the first time. 'He was such a dear. He had such high principles.' As Deans have, thought Emily. 'His voice – so rich, so reassuring. We all miss him so much.' They all looked at his photograph as if by looking at it they might conjure him up. The ringing in Emily's ears was louder. Perhaps she was going deaf.

'This is such a nice light room,' they said, changing the subject. 'And what a wonderful view. You can smell the spray even in here, and the seagulls come so close and look so huge. Nothing between you and the cliffs – not another house in sight.'

Emily wished at times that she was a seagull plunging and wheeling over the cliffs and down into the sea at will.

On her next morning walk she did manage to get a little nearer the edge, which felt exciting, like a shot of adrenalin. It was raining and the grass was slippery. Closer, she thought, closer. She could just see over the edge. She could feel her heart battering as if to batter its way out of her mouth.

This was the sort of thing she did not want to tell the sorceress, who liked to question her.

'Tell me about yourself,' she insisted.

Oh not all that again, thought Emily. I'm so fagged out.

'Otherwise you are simply a cipher.'

Oh no, no, thought Emily. I can't bear to be that. 'I have this ringing in my ears,' she said.

'What is it you don't want to hear?' The sorceress was inspecting her gardener's nails. 'What do you want me to do?'

'Wave a wand I suppose,' Emily spoke rather rudely.

The sorceress went out of the room and returned with a small phial of oil. Emily was struck with unexpected pleasure as she breathed in the perfume of millions of rose beds, miles of lavender fields, cascades of orange blossom.

'This part of the hand is called the Palace of Anxieties,' said the sorceress as she smoothed the oil into the very centre of the widow's palm, that part of the palm which has a little well in it.

'Ah,' sighed Emily, and the sorceress beamed in delight.

She gave Emily the rest of the oil to take home.

'Sprinkle it around you at night,' she said. 'Let the scent waft over you as you turn in your sleep.'

But that night Emily was so tired when she went to bed she forgot to do what the sorceress had told her.

She fell into a dream. She was in a tall building. It was called the Palace of Anxieties. She was climbing the spiral staircase. She came to a door which was painted, or rather smeared with red. 'Come in Petal,' said a far away voice. 'I'm just having my tea.' Emily went in and sat down. There was a table spread with scones and a pot of jam and those little biscuits called jammy dodgers. The food was not real – it was play food. It was a pretend tea party.

'When you've finished your tea,' said the sorceress who seemed to have seagull's wings. 'When you've quite finished, I'll show you the torture chamber.'

'Oh good.' Emily was being brave.

'And all the paraphernalia.'

'Oh good.' She was brazening it out.

'And then you can decide – one way or the other.'

They sat pretending to drink their tea and eat the scones and biscuits.

Then the sorceress said, the atmosphere meanwhile thinning with terror. 'If you've finished, Petal . . .'

Emily thought she would be taken down to the room where such things as man traps were kept but instead she found herself in a small room with a skylight in the ceiling. Seagulls screamed outside the glass and flew off suddenly. The room looked neat and medical. There was a couch with a lamp over it. The sorceress pulled a wad of cottonwool out of a box and covered her own mouth with it, hooking the tapes over her ears. It kept falling off and she kept putting it back. It muffled her voice. 'Take your shoes off; Petal, and get up on the bed. Take your time now, we're not in a race.' She flicked on the overhead lamp and began to knead and scrape down each side of Petal's spine with a scooping movement as if scooping out the flesh.

'You have to be cruel to be kind,' she said. 'Turn over now on to your back.' Petal turned over and shielded her eyes from the glare of the lamp.

Emily woke from this dream suddenly and with a stiff back. She had gone to sleep with the bedside light on and now it was morning. Carefully, so as not to fall giddily, she got out of bed and went over to draw back the curtains on to pale sunshine and the whirling seagulls banging their wings on the glass and calling her to the cliff edge.

Emily did not bother to dress. She put the Dean's cloak over her thin nightdress and so did not feel the early morning chill, but the sharp gravel hurt her feet as she ran down the path, crocus lighting her way like small torches.

She went straight to the edge of the cliff. The seagulls swooped to show her how easy it was. They screamed at her excitedly. Emily. Emily.

Perhaps if she took a run and jump, instead of just dropping, wings would quickly sprout and spread out like an opening sail.

She began walking back from the edge, her giddiness making her stumble; it had never been so bad – it must be part of the beginning to fly business. Perhaps seagulls were permanently giddy. She could feel wings beginning to prick her shoulders as if sharp feathers broke through. The soles of her feet itched as she turned back to face the edge. It was all part of what was going to happen. She was ready in her bare feet to make a run at it.

Then as one might suddenly see a mushroom in the grass that had not been there before, she saw in the near distance the figure of her husband the Dean. She knew it was him at once – he had his head held in that characteristic way as if listening.

He was standing there weighing up the jump he was about to take. He was not going to take a run at it – he was just going to jump.

Now Emily the Dean's wife tried to cry out, 'Wait for me,'

but her voice would not come, she only heard the words in her head. She began flying to him over the wet grass. Flying. She flew to his side and was there in an amazingly short time. He turned and saw her. 'Don't try to stop me,' he said quite kindly. He looked freezing cold. She took the cloak off and put it round his shoulders. For a moment he stood there looking as he had always looked. She held on to his cloak, but he suddenly slipped out of it and disappeared over the edge leaving the cloak in her hands.

She stood listening to the silence in which the occasional bird screamed.

After a while she put the cloak over her own shoulders and trudged home.

'Well that's a nice heavy cloak,' said the sorceress. 'But warm for the time of the year.'

'I'm going on a journey,' said Emily. 'It stands up to all weathers.'

'Ah,' said the sorceress. 'I will give you something for your journey.' She gave Emily a phial of oils.

'I have some already,' said Emily. 'I sprinkle it around me at night.'

'This is different.'

Emily undid the stopper. She smelled gorse and sea and something else.

'Is it a love potion?' she asked.

'Yes of course,' said the sorceress.

Emily got out her cheque book. 'No need for a card,' said the sorceress graciously.

'Goodbye then,' said Emily.

She made her way down the stone steps her cloak trailing on the ground, for the Dean had been quite tall. As she drove off, her few things for the journey in the back of the car, she threw the cloak on to the back seat. It was a warm sunny spring morning but the climate was precarious and she might be away – well she did not know how long it would be.

There was a queue for the ferry and she sat patiently waiting listening to her car radio playing Bach – this was accompanied by the faint cries of the sea-birds. A holiday the doctor had said. A love affair perhaps.

It was all going to be marvellous. There were plenty of cliffs around the Isle of Wight – she would have a choice. As she drove on to the car deck and felt the throb of the ship's engines she thought, I'm off. Flying. She would stand on the edge of the sheerest cliff she could find. She would fly. She would disappear. She would drop into the arms of her lover.

'Where are the best cliffs?' she asked a sailor as she drove off the car deck.

'Try Freshwater,' he said.

She stopped the car and looked for Freshwater on the map. When she got to a place called Blackgang she had to take the military road. It was certainly a lovely day for it. 'Nowhere's very far on the island,' the sailor had said.

When she got there she found the sheer cliffs were only yards from the road. No one seemed worried by this. A daredevil couple were sitting dangling their legs over the edge. Children and dogs raced about in the sunshine.

She would have to wait for nightfall.

She found a large flat stone to sit on, and wait. While waiting she took out her phial of oil, the love potion, and sniffed it gingerly. It smelled no different from the gorse and thyme-scented salt air. That was a bit odd – it had been quite expensive. For some reason Emily found this amusing and laughed to herself, but she rubbed some into her palms anyway.

'Those people shouldn't be on the edge like that,' said a small boy, 'they'll go overboard, my dad said so. Why are you sitting on a stone?'

'Is that your dog?' Emily pointed to the exuberant young golden retriever.

'Yes,' said the boy, racing off. 'He's called Brian,' he called over his shoulder.

Emily's leg went into a cramp and she stood up. She was hungry, she suddenly realised, really uncomfortably hungry. She thought about people having a last meal. A well fried mackerel with brown bread. A nice ripe pear. A piece of sharp crumbly cheese.

'Is there a café round here?' she asked the dare-devil couple. She peered over the cliff edge as she spoke. The sea below was several shades of lapis lazuli and jade.

The café was too far away to walk, they said, and it would only be open for about another hour.

She found the café. It was a wooden hut almost buried in gorse. She had never seen gorse that shone so bright. Emily's hunger made every mouthful of the cheese a real pleasure. 'What do you do for pleasure?' the sorceress had asked her more than once. There was no one else in the café except her and the girl who brought her food.

'Staying?' the girl asked her, plonking down a jug of water on the table.

'Staying?'

'Staying hereabouts?'

'Oh no I'm not staying.'

The girl went and stood behind the counter, tidying up at the end of the day. She put things away but left the bowl of fruit in the centre of the counter as a decoration. The appleness of the apples streamed out, it meant something ungraspable, strange, beyond thought. And there was an orange, large, deep coloured. No strawberries.

The girl brought coffee and the bill and put it down on the table. The blue oilskin tablecloth shone like the sea, the heavy white crockery floating on it. Emily noticed with a shock that under the girl's silver bracelets were other bracelets of red inflamed scars, and at once felt she must hear her story.

The girl turned the notice round to close the place and sat down to tell her story, which was a commonplace one of love and betrayal. Her dark eyelashes lowered in her downcast gaze were of such beauty and lustre, and her story was indeed so everyday yet unique, that Emily was pierced with love for her.

The cliffs and seagulls, the sky, sea and flowers, the golden retriever dog and the little boy, the sailor and the dare-devil couple, the Mothers Union ladies and the sorceress herself all sang together for everyone and everything that was alive at this moment.

The girl's hair now fell over her face as she finished her story.

Emily saw in her mind's eye the girl running to the cliff edge, her dark hair streaming behind her. 'Take this,' she said. It was the phial of oil, the love potion.

Warily the girl took it and sniffed it. 'It smells of primroses,' she said. 'Just picked.'

'It's different for everyone,' said Emily. 'Take it, keep it. I've finished with it.'

SAVED BY THE BELL

~

Beryl Roberts

Miss Eleanor Harris, Head of Middle School and teacher of Religious Studies at Wood End Comprehensive School, gazes out of her study window on the school's third floor, which gives her an uninterrupted aerial view of the school's tennis courts and ramshackle bicycle-sheds. The late autumnal day is cold and grey. Leaves hang like limp flags from the dull clump of trees that forms the school's natural boundary and gives the school its name, but the combined greyness of sky and concrete yard is broken by maroon uniform-clad Lowreyesque figures below which radiate ever-changing patterns, as if they are pieces being shaken within a gigantic kaleidoscope. It's always the same, muses Miss Harris, the clusters of pupils talking animatedly are always the girls and the bodies hurtling around, pushing, pummelling and yelling are invariably the boys.

Suddenly, the piercing shrill of the electric bell signalling morning registration causes a temporary silence and an unnatural freezing of movement, but by the third blast, bunches of excited, shouting teenagers mob the entrance doors to the school, where the teacher on duty makes a half-hearted attempt to assert control and order. Just like Pavlov's dogs, thinks Miss Harris. Every day potential anarchy looms in every school, kept dormant only by a collective response to timed bells.

From her window, Miss Harris sees and hears Doug King, a member of the Physical Education Department and form teacher of the notorious Form 10X, lumbering complainingly on to cloakroom duty, his leg muscles stretching taut his green nylon and lycra tracksuit bottoms, his bulging calves and thighs like two pods of broad beans, his beer belly over-lapping the waistband. He struggles, visibly, to reason with the chattering, cheeky bodies his fingers itch to pinch and prod into submission with the tactics he uses in the scrum every Saturday. The boys know he is on a permanent short fuse, so they try to rile him, egging on 'King Kong', as they call him out of ear-shot, to rattle the cage bars, taunting his muscle-bound brain with a cunning mixture of gestural and silent defiance.

'Come on now, single file. You know the rules,' he shouts, expecting to be ignored. He recognises a smiling face bobbing past him and bellows in an ear, 'I hear you scored a blinder on Saturday, Richards. Well done!' He turns to face the anonymous blur of faces.

'Stop pushing and you'll get in faster!' he yells.

A minor deviation in someone's uniform hits him in the practised eye like a pellet from a catapult. He waves his arms.

'Hey, you! Yes, you! Come back here!'

A youth fights against the tide of heaving bodies to return to Doug King's side.

'I might have known it was you, Mann!'

'What sir? What have I done?'

Pupils giggle as they push past.

'Dave Mann? More like Cave-Man.' Doug King leers at his own wit. Miss Harris watches the boy flinch as Doug King's guffaw sends gusts of pure nicotine fumes into his face. 'You're trying to wind me up, aren't you? Go on, admit it.'

'No, sir.'

More giggles.

'Well, what do you think you're doing coming to school in *that*?' He stares goggle-eyed at the offending garment.

Dave Mann affects a look of innocence. 'In what, sir?'

Bristles rise on the back of Doug King's short, thick neck.

'Never mind, "What, sir?" You know what.' He prods an inch of contrast colour on the boy's chest with a knobbly finger. 'No logos allowed on school sweaters.'

There's an eyeball-to-eyeball moment of crisis.

'My school sweater's in the wash, sir.'

'You've had the whole weekend to get it washed.'

'The washing machine broke down, sir. Nothing we could do.'

'Well you can't wear that one around school, or we'll have an outbreak of designer labels appearing. What do you think this is, a catwalk? Take it off!'

'It's too cold, sir, and the radiators don't work in half the classrooms anyway.'

Doug King thinks back to his invigilation of an A' Level re-sit examination held in a requisitioned Portakabin the previous week, when he'd been forced to drape himself, physically, along a radiator just to keep his circulation going. He had had no idea how the examinees had been able to control their frozen hands to write. He concedes, silently, that the boy has a valid point.

No more bodies push past. Heavy, shoe-scuffed outer swing-doors clash shut. Doug King consults his watch and decides to pursue a quick cup of coffee in preference to a dubious, protracted victory over logos. He knocks the power-ritual defensively into touch by insisting upon the last word.

'Well, I haven't got time to deal with you. Report to Miss Harris. Tell her Mr King sent you.'

Dave Mann manages to look suitably demure. With a bit of luck, looking for Miss Harris might mean missing Assembly in the Main Hall, a twice-weekly pain in the groin.

'Yes, sir.'

'Well, go on then. *Move!*'

Mr King sprints the steps leading to the first-floor staff-room, while Dave Mann, smiling knowingly, moves leisurely across the yard under Miss Harris's window. From experience she is able to trace the youth's movements, and even time, within seconds, his knocking at her door. He'll dawdle, probably visit the toilet on the first floor, where he'll smoke half a cigarette, before climbing the final stairs to her room. There he'll pause to adopt an injured expression, catch his breath, then knock at her door.

Miss Harris looks at the door, imagining the fist curling the other side preparing to thump it soundly. Instead, her telephone rings. She lifts the receiver. A voice rasps. It is the man she still refers to as 'the new Headmaster', though he is now into his fourth term at the school. She senses from the strained civility of the tone and the forced friendliness that he is not alone; he is playing to the gallery, acting casual and controlled to impress his audience. His voice is oily with effort.

'Ah, Eleanor?'

Her own name spoken by an enemy does not belong to her. It warrants no response.

'Eleanor, are you there?' The tone becomes already a little impatient.

She is tempted to join in the charade by replying, 'No,' but she does not know whom he is with and she decides to play safe.

She jumps. 'Yes, sorry! I think there is someone at my door waiting to see me.'

'Well, I won't keep you a minute. I just wanted to tell you that I'll be bringing a visitor into your Assembly this morning.'

She senses a trick. She feels an involuntary chill.

'*My* Assembly?'

She is confused but she remains calm, then she peers myopically at her notice board and runs her finger horizontally along the day's duty roster. She sees in clear type 'Monday, November 10th Assembly in Main Hall. Years 8-10: Miss Harris.' Her finger touches the caked correcting fluid proud on the surface of the roster. She realises, with sinking spirits, that the list has been altered since she last checked it at Friday lunch-time, and that only one person in the school has the motive and the power to risk that type of intimidation. She wonders what they do in other places, when it's suspected that the biggest school bully is the Headmaster.

'The visitor is Mr Crawford, our newly designated H.M.I. He doesn't begin his official duties until after Christmas but he's raring to get to know us. He has a special responsibility for School Assemblies, and I think he'll enjoy one of your classics. We'll be down in about ten minutes.'

She knows he is smirking now, sensing his own triumph and her blind panic at having to face three hundred bored teenagers, a dozen critical teachers and an expectant government inspector with absolutely nothing to say.

The telephone goes dead. There is a knock at her door and, at her command, Dave Mann sidles his way in insolently. He blurts out his message, while her eyes scan him from head to foot. The logo stitched on the left side of the sweater is innocuous. Nevertherless, school uniform rules are non-negotiable. She tells the youth, quite calmly, that he has a choice of either removing the sweater immediately, or of being sent home with a letter to his parents reminding them of the contract they entered into when they applied for their son to be admitted as a pupil there. Dave Mann is taken aback. She hasn't remonstrated, reprimanded, or threatened. She has merely stated her intention to involve his parents. He doesn't think it's fair. He reckons she's not playing the game. Problems in school end nebulously, daily on the final bell; those taken home fester, create multiple inconveniences and repercussions like cuts in pocket money, late night curfews, a ban on weekend stop-overs at friends' houses. He wants to provoke an argument with this old bat, who doesn't play according to the book, but her face has closed. He does not realise how fast and furiously her brain is working at survival, so he misinterprets her set facial expression. He concedes defeat, tugs off his sweater, which he throws defiantly at her feet, and storms out of the room and down the stairs. He feels justified in skipping Assembly in favour of having a smoke.

Another bell signals the movement of classes to the Main Hall for Assembly. Miss Harris walks down two flights of stairs, as if in a dream, and crosses the wind-swept yard towards the main entrance, where rows of maroon figures inch forward like giant arteries pumping life into the grey building. She sees the Headmaster standing with his guest, ready to sweep majestically into the hall to witness her humiliation. The two men, although only recently introduced, chat animatedly like old friends, so they do not see her dithering nervously. Suddenly, instinctively, she knows what to do.

She strides confidently into the ground-floor cloakroom area. She often makes random forays into little-known, dusty niches, catching smokers hiding in toilets hoping to dodge Assemblies. On one occasion, she had startled a pick-pocket rifling among the hanging outer coats, her hands full of money. Another time, she had caught two Year 11 pupils discovering sex, uncomfortably, on a pile of lost-property clothing dumped in a corner. Her presence there today excites no particular interest.

She checks there is no one in sight, then she positions

herself close to the wall from which protrudes a domed, glass panel covering a fire-alarm. She removes her shoe, hits the glass with force and watches it shatter. Louder, even than the pounding of her own heartbeat, rises the strident scream of the fire-bell; there is a cheer from bolder pupils who sense a prankster at work, then the flow of maroon bodies gushes from the Main Hall like an enormous haemorrhage, out on to the tennis courts, the designated assembly points for all school fire-drills.

Miss Harris joins the mass of pupils filing out, and begins disciplining them, because they are noisy and boisterous, thrilled, as she herself is, at having avoided the ordeal of her Assembly. Everyone assumes the fire bell is a hoax. Now begins the search for the culprit. An example must be made. A breach of discipline and safety must be punished. Form teachers bustle officiously up and down rows of pupils, consulting class registers and checking class numbers. Only one pupil is found to be missing: Dave Mann.

'Typical! Bloody typical!' moans Doug King, his form-master, predicting hours of police-type investigations ahead.

The roll-call complete, files of maroon-clad figures are allowed back into the building for the start of morning lessons. Miss Harris catches up with the new Headmaster and the H.M.I. as she seeks the sanctuary of her own room. She overhears the H.M.I. speaking heatedly to the Headmaster, criticising the low efficiency of the drill and the faulty evacuation procedures. She hears snatches of sentences 'dangerously slow reaction', 'lack of discipline' and 'need to report this to the Office when I get back.' He breaks off the harangue to acknowledge Miss Harris, as she passes. He seems disappointed to have missed her Assembly and tells her kindly that he will find an early opportunity to revisit the school to get to know her better.

He sees the bright eyes and nervous smile of the faded woman in front of him and he feels genuinely sorry that some mindless prankster has robbed her of a chance to impress him with a well-prepared moral message. The Headmaster looks ruffled; his lips purse in disappointment but he lacks the imagination to suspect her.

Miss Harris feels for the first time in her life the thrill of lawlessness and, as she collides in a corridor with Dave Mann shivering in his shirt-sleeves, being frog-marched for questioning by the scowling Doug King, she gives the boy what he could have sworn was a furtive wink.

THE NOTORIOUS DAUGHTERS OF VENUS

~

Ceri Jordan

'It's a scandal,' Cati Jones announced, folding her broad arms
across her equally broad chest as if to repel some imaginary
and long-hoped-for affront to her modesty. 'An absolute
scandal. How are we ever to hold our heads up at the County
WI Conference again?'

Mrs Walther settled for a long, slow shake of her head, and
squinted out at the rain showering from the eaves. She'd only
popped into the Post Office for a bag of sugar and an Air
Mail Printed Paper to Indonesia. Martin loved his monthly
bundle of local press cuttings. At least, that's what he kept
saying in those bizarre e-mail things he sent via the shoe
factory's computer. Reminded him of home, he said. If she
could keep him that eager to hear about the local drink-
driving figures and all his old schoolfriends' marriages, she
reasoned, he'd have to come home one day.

'I mean, every village for miles has got one. Pentrecynnon,
they had those lady highwaymen for a start. All right, that
was a couple of hundred years back, but their house is still
standing, you know. There's even a little plaque outside. And
there was Mrs Bradley in Tollfar, murdered her husband and
seventeen wedding guests besides – and nearly got away
with it, too. Would have if she hadn't kept the packaging the
pastrami came in and the police realised it wasn't out of date
at all . . .'

Mrs Walther nodded dismally.

'And here's us. Felinffarn, largest and oldest village in

125

the whole valley, Best Kept in Dyfed four times running. And when the man from Notorious Women of the Terefi Valley arrives today, looking for things to put in his book, what will he find? Old Mrs Penry with a criminal record for animal rights demonstrations, and one teenager excluded for getting confused and trying to smoke the kind of grass you grow on your lawns, that's what!'

Scowling at the downpour that was hindering her long-overdue escape, Mrs Walther muttered, 'If you're that worried, Cati, why don't you just make something up?'

The words must have had a considerable effect. Cati actually stopped talking for a few seconds.

Then the spell wore off, and she said slowly, thoughtfully; 'About who, though?'

'Doesn't have to be about anyone who's here now. Make up some old legend.' Groping desperately for something that would beat the lady highwaymen and their plaque, she found herself saying, 'A lady cannibal or something. They got up to all sorts of weird things in those days.'

Cati shook her head slowly. 'No. We'll never get the first chapter in the book with some old legend. What we need is someone still alive who we can make things up about and they'll never know. Someone who never comes out much, someone who won't answer the door when he goes round to check their side of the story.'

And Mrs Walther realised they were both looking in the same direction. Up through the grey blur of the rain towards the equally grey outline of Waterloo House, a dismal full stop at the end of the snaking farm track that climbed the steep east face of Ffynnon Hill.

'Like the daughters of Venus.'

'That's what they're called round here. The Daughters of

Venus,' Cati declared, looking sharply round the café as if defying anyone to contradict her. No one did. Mrs Walther had obviously spread the word more enthusiastically than her permanent scowl had suggested she would.

The Man From The Book – a Mr Millidge, with floppy brown hair and wire-rimmed glasses under an Indiana Jones hat – nodded and made a few more squiggles in his notebook. He had a tape recorder on the table between them, sandwiched between the scones and the teapot, but he obviously didn't trust it. She was still careful to address herself to the machine, though, and not to him. He might end up selling tapes, like those audio-books you get from the library, and she wanted to be quite sure she was presenting herself at her best.

After a clatter of plates from the counter had died away, Mr Millidge scratched his eyebrow with the end of his pencil and asked her, 'Why, exactly?'

'Well, their mother was called . . . But mostly, well, you know. Two women living in the same house, never married, bit suspicious, isn't it?'

'You did say they're sisters . . .?'

Cati leant closer, dropping her voice to a low and deadly whisper. 'Which makes it all the worse, wouldn't you say?'

Mr Millidge From The Book nodded absently, spilling tea into his saucer as he picked up the cup. He didn't exactly look riveted. A quick glance round at the other customers – Carly sniggering into her brushed silk sleeve, a shirt far too dressy for taking tea with her elderly mother if you asked Cati; and there, the Misses Abnett, whispering behind their hands – and she knew she was going to have to resort to desperate measures.

'Alone, that is, since the strange disappearance of Joni Shenkin.'

Mr Millidge's grey eyes widened, just a little, and he set the teacup down again.

'Joni Shenkin, you see, he had a thing about Gwen. Younger by a year, Gwen, and you can be sure that Jan dominated her life since the moment she was born. So, there was no way that she'd put up with Joni being up there all hours of the day and night, with flowers and cards and all.'

The Misses Abnett were looking at her in absolute horror, but she knew they wouldn't contradict it. Not since she saw them skinny-dipping that night with Tom Carter, who was thirty-five if he was a day, and if their poor mother knew how friendly he was with the pair of them – the pair of them, mind – the shock would send her to her grave . . .

Mr Millidge was just staring at her, waiting.

'So one night – this was about twenty years ago, mind, I was only a girl – Joni Shenkin goes up there to visit Gwen. Never comes home. The next morning, the postman found the flowers he'd been carrying all scattered in the front garden, scattered and trampled. And Joni Shenkin was never seen round here again.'

Well, she added mentally; apart from the train guard he bought the ticket to Cardiff from, and the half-dozen people who saw him on the platform. And the people of Cardiff, and that girl from Nigeria he married in the end, once he'd got over whatever Gwen told him that night – but she'd quite deliberately said he was never seen round here again, so they didn't count.

Mr Millidge frowned at the crumbs on his plate as if they were evidence of some terrible indiscretion. 'Didn't the police . . .?'

'Oh, they looked around, but in the end they said the evidence wasn't conclusive. His pocket watch was lying on their garden path, but he could have dropped it as he was leaving.

His bank account was closed a few days later, by post, all his savings drawn out, but he could have done that himself. If he'd run off somewhere. Even the blood on their sofa could have been what they said it was – he cut himself on the cake knife while they were having some supper together.'

Mr Millidge swallowed hard, and made a few more squiggles in the notebook.

Damn. She should never have mentioned the blood. She'd have to make absolutely sure he didn't go up there now. They'd had the same sofa for fifty years, the one their mother was given at her wedding, and there was never so much as a speck of dust on it, let alone a stain that might pass for blood.

'The thing is,' Mr Millidge said slowly, biting the end of his pencil between words, 'this does pretty much amount to hearsay. Without any evidence . . .'

Cati sat back in her chair, scrabbling frantically for something else to pin on them. There had to be something. Graffiti was pretty pointless, who was worried about that? Theft was a bit common. Happened all the time. There hadn't been any sudden deaths recently, not even animals, what was she going to tell him now . . .?

Of course.

'And then,' she said, very softly, aware of the utter hushed silence in the teashop as everyone strained to hear the latest progeny of her fertile mind, 'there's the black magic coven of Terefi Tor.'

The Tor was a fair walk, even for a young man like him, and he was flushed and panting when they reached the top and stood blinking into the gritty wind, the whole valley spread out below them.

The river was only a silver strip from up here, edged by dark green; the fields beyond, paler and thinly-sown. At the junction of the two, the path up to Waterloo House began. Cati squinted down at the turning, scanning the stile, the gate, the few wilted bushes that almost hid the road sign.

No sign that Mrs Walther had actually made it yet. Well, she was just going to have to hope.

'Well,' Mr Millidge coughed, finally catching his breath. 'I don't claim to be any expert, mind you, but don't black masses normally happen at night?'

Cati opened her mouth, and closed it again before anything incriminating could escape. 'Ah. This is a sort of preparatory thing. Preparing herself for the actual black mass. You wouldn't catch me out here when they're actually involved in that sort of stuff, oh no— '

Far, far below, the bushes rustled, and a figure swathed in black stepped uncertainly into view, picking her way fastidiously between two rows of Mark Dewitt's prize organic beetroot.

Cati smiled.

Mrs Walther scowled at the field of beet spread out before her, and wondered if this wasn't taking things a little too far. She hadn't minded helping out fabricating that story about the Headless Horseman for *Chilling Tales from Chilly Wales*, of course, because that was just a story. Hadn't got them anywhere, anyway. The editor had said that headless horsemen were terribly passé darlings, and they had never made it past the Other Locations section in the index. Mrs Walther had been a little surprised by that. It had never occurred to her that ghosts had to keep up with the times.

And now, here she was. Dressed in old Mrs Stevens' widow's weeds (four times used, and starting to look it), and a hastily dyed net curtain, prancing around a field to convince some bored hack that two harmless old dears were baby-sacrificing lunatics.

She should never have told Cati about those incriminating photos, that was the root of it. If she'd only kept her mouth shut, she wouldn't have to keep indulging the woman's communal delusions of grandeur . . .

What was it she was supposed to be doing? Oh, that's right.

Fishing in her pocket, she found the pocket flask of Ribena and produced it with what she hoped was a suitably demonic flourish.

'What's she got there?' Mr Millidge demanded, squinting into the sun.

Cati pressed the opera glasses hastily into his hand, hoping he wouldn't notice the faded PROPERTY OF RHYL PAVILION on the underside. 'Here. Maybe you can make it out. My eyes aren't what they used to be, you know.'

Mrs Walther was prancing along the beetroot rows with gay abandon now, scattering dilute Ribena in all directions. It didn't look the right colour from here, not with the naked eye, but hopefully Mr Millidge didn't usually get close enough to these notorious women he was so interested in to be sure what precise shade blood was.

A moment of held breath; then Mr Millidge gasped and lowered the opera glasses as if shying from some terrible sight. 'My God. I think she's . . . worshipping something.'

Snatching the glasses from his limp and clammy hand, Cati clamped them to her eyes.

Mrs Walther had fallen over. In that depth of mud, she was going to be a while getting up, and those widow's weeds certainly weren't going to be fit to honour the demise of the current Mr Stevens.

'That's it,' she announced, seizing Mr Millidge by the arm and spinning him round like a top. 'I'm not going to stay in sight of her a second longer. The Lord alone knows what might happen— '

She couldn't have timed it better herself.

Engrossed in the squirming devotions to some earth god that Mrs Walther appeared to be performing between the now-mangled beetroot, they hadn't even noticed the clouds slinking up the valley from the coast. Now, as they turned to face a sky the colour of tarnished brass, lightening split it from top to bottom, and buried itself in the bushes edging the beet field.

Mr Millidge let out a shriek that must have been heard from there to Pentrecynnon, and bolted away down the path like all the fiends of Hell were following on his tail.

Cati sneaked a look back at the beetroot field. Energised – mercifully, not literally – by the near miss, Mrs Walther had found her way back to her feet and was scuttling towards the gate, waving her arms in the air like a frightened dervish.

Hmm. All in all, that had been rather successful, really.

The book came out on the Friday, available over the counter at the Post Office 'as a special service to our customers'. And on the Monday morning, the police arrived.

From her bedroom window, the spare bedroom with the primrose print curtains and the view all the way up the valley, Mrs Walther watched the two vans wind their way up Ffynnon Hill and pull into the cobbled yard of Waterloo House. The officers were in full riot gear, and even from here, she could tell they'd made a real mess of knocking the front door down. The whole door frame would have to be replaced, and that would cost, wouldn't it?

Watching them bundle the startled old dears into the back of the van, handcuffed and trembling, Mrs Walther felt a momentary twinge of conscience. But then again. The police would soon work out it was all nonsense, all that stuff in the book about child sacrifices and strange chanting heard on the hills at solstices. Of course they would. And Jan and Gwen probably hadn't had this much fun for years.

Anyway, it made her feel a little better about all the lies they'd told to dear silly Mr Millidge. In the end, it had turned out just to be a change of identity. Like on those TV programmes where all names have been changed to protect the innocent. Or in this case, the guilty.

In the end, it wasn't a lie at all. There were plenty of notorious women in Felinffarn. Liars and cheats and blackmailers and schemers. It was just that the daughters of Venus Spencer weren't among them.

Mrs Walther glanced across the valley, towards the low grey-brick outline of the Post Office.

Perhaps Mr Millidge would consider a new chapter for the second edition.

VOODOO CANTATA

~

G. P. Hughes

Life is full of surprises and here is one of them: at the age of 43 I have been transformed – from a polite and soft-spoken housewife who would not drown a spider in the bath – to a lucid and dangerous woman. This didn't happen overnight. For years I peered through a curtain of rain and despaired as my son Fred trudged up the path, his head bowed under the weight of his fatherless condition. I couldn't believe our situation would ever change. But now I see that all my years of silent suffering were but a mute rehearsal, a preparation for the new woman to come.

Making a decision is the first step to success. From the day I decided to place myself in the hands of an alternative therapist, my destiny was revealed. I was suffering from breathing problems: at first only when climbing hills but gradually the breathlessness got worse and worse till I'd wake in the night as if someone were throttling me. The pills doled out by the NHS only increased my heart rate, depressed my psyche and added pounds.

In desperation, I went to see Madame Phyllis, who was advertised in the *Caernarfon and Denbigh Herald*. She was jocular and sun-tanned. Her piercing blue eyes took me in and she announced: 'You've worked very hard to develop a nice soft voice, a reserved exterior that nobody can object to. But inside there's a powerful woman, raging to emerge. Does that make sense?'

It did. I was amazed how she could see so far into my soul.

I told Madame Phyllis about my ex-husband Gerald, how he'd left me and son Fred and gone off to Baltimore, Maryland, and married Norma, the daughter of a wealthy garment manufacturer, how the old man gives them air miles so they can spend every summer in Europe. But they never visit me and Fred.

Gerald always said he was an exiled member of the royal family of Albania and I believed him. He was my first and only love and I still regard him as a miracle. He came walking into the London squat where I lived just when I was almost resigned to the fact that because of my skin, which is pockmarked from teenage acne, and my thick glasses, I'd remain a virgin forever. We got married the week after we met because Gerald was on a drugs charge and the Home Office was trying to deport him.

At first we were blissfully happy. But after Fred was born, everything changed. Gerald started staying out late, drinking. Then my Auntie Vi in Bermuda died, leaving me a small inheritance. When Gerald got wind of it, he began demanding money. I could hear Auntie Vi: 'Come on, Cleo, get a grip. Put the money where that s.o.b can't get his greasy meathooks on it!'

I knew she was right. The dirt and fumes of London didn't seem a proper environment for a baby anyway so, like a cat dragging her kittens out of danger, I removed Gerald and Fred by train to Snowdonia. The day after we arrived, whilst pushing Fred along a lane hemmed by crumbling stone walls, we came upon a dilapidated cottage surrounded by cypress and cedar, birch and rowan. A 'For Sale' sign waved miraculously.

It was love at first sight. With the garden, that is. I'd reckoned without the house. Try as I might, I've never been able to eradicate the mould that sprouts with the autumn rains, nor banish the rats gnawing at our kitchen floor-boards. If Gerald had stayed, we might have tackled these problems together. But he soon got fed up with the wind and the wet nappies, the tee-totalling, bell-clanging Sundays. He was off.

Me, I've discovered a certain affinity with wind and heather, with the light after rain, sparkling on the quarry. And my Fred, despite his honey-coloured skin, has become a proper Welshman with a gogish accent and a fine singing voice. But the point is, we seldom hear from his father – only the occasional postcard from Aculpoco or Paris, France.

I am not a grasping woman but I wish Gerald would shoulder some of the responsibility. Now that Fred's a strapping lad of six foot two, quite frankly, my larder is almost always bare. He can't go work in the quarry because he's only 13. I can't set the Child Support Agency on Gerald while he's in America. My pittance from the DSS barely covers coal and the fiver I get off Mrs Jones for cleaning is quickly devoured by Manweb.

I say: why should Fred be deprived while his father lives in the lap of luxury? It's not fair. Fred's a clever lad. If only Gerald and Norma would pause, as they consume their air miles, to consider his plight. But no. Fred does not exist in their eyes.

All this I told to Madame Phyllis who traced an elegant index finger along the arch of her eyebrow as I talked. At last she said, 'You're consumed with anger against your husband Gerald. That's what's throttling you.'

Because I have never, not even when Fred was naughty as a youngster, raised my voice in anger, I was very surprised. But Madame Phyllis shook her finger. 'You're turning your anger inwards,' she warned. 'It could be very damaging for you.'

'But what can I do?' I cried.

'Pound a pillow and pretend it's Gerald,' she said, eyes gleaming ferociously. 'It's time to release your shackles!'

Then she handed me the pamphlet which has changed my life: 'Auto-Therapy for the Over-Stressed: No. 5, Do-it-yourself Revenge.'

As the bus bounced through the potholes on the way up to Cwm Hyfryd, I read the pamphlet. It was a revelation! The author, Mandy B, was a woman just like me. She too had suffered the dark nights of disappointed love, the agonies of bereavement, until one day in the public library when the remedy for anger and sorrow came to her. Voodoo. A simple and effective technique for bringing peace to the user. Voodoo. The word tingled along my spine. And then it hit me. What she could do, I could do.

Just make a doll, said Mandy B, and stick pins in strategic places. I'd pretend it was Gerald. Or should it be Norma? The purpose was to release stress and anger in the user, not to harm other people. I read on. There were recipes for making your love return and also for causing boils on a rival's back-side. There was even a Celtic curse handed down through 2000 years of oral tradition. By the time I arrived in Cwm Hyfryd, I'd devoured the pamphlet from cover to cover.

'You look very happy, Mam,' Fred said over dinner. 'Can I take the telly to me room?' Now, normally I'd have lectured him before giving in but that night I couldn't wait to be alone.

Gerald's old blue shirt with the yellow stars was still in the closet. I took the large gingerbread cutter from the kitchen drawer and cut two shapes which I stitched together. Stuff with rue, said Mandy B, but all I had was a jar of mixed herbs so I used that. When the doll was nicely plump, I took the snapshot of Gerald and me leaving the Finsbury Park

Registry Office on our wedding day and pinned it through its
heart. He looked so handsome in his lizardskin winklepickers
and borrowed tuxedo. He was bending down to kiss me and
one of my pigtails caressed his shoulder. Tears flooded my
eyes but I quickly brushed them away. Get a grip, Cleo. What
I had to do now was keep up the meditation for seven days.
But I thought I'd give it a fortnight, considering Gerald was
overseas.

The next morning I decided it was only fair to inform him
that I had taken matters into my own hands, so, 'Dear
Gerald,' I wrote, 'I can't go on like this any longer. Fred is
heartbroken that you don't care. His coat is in tatters and his
wellies are too small. I have kept your memory alive as long
as possible but the time has come for drastic action. Yours,
Cleo.'

Before I'd even memorised the homecoming chant, a reply
plopped through the door: 'Dear Cleo,' it said, 'On June 15th,
Gerald and I will be stopping at Heathrow en route to the
Venice Biennial. We plan to drop in on Fred so Gerald can do
some bonding. Can you please reserve a room with double
bed for that night? A Travel Lodge would be suitable but any
three-star hotel will do. Norma.'

My legs turned to jelly. To be honest, I hadn't believed the
spell would work. But Norma's letter was proof. And right
was on my side. Yes! Simple repetition was all I needed. I
would not fail. The intensity of my love would bring Gerald
back to me.

On the morning of the 15th, I dusted the bedroom, changed
the sheets and emptied two drawers of the dresser. Then I
ran a deep bath and pondered my dilemma. According to
Mandy B, a relaxing bath was the perfect place for an effective

and heartfelt curse. But for Gerald or for Norma? It was Gerald who was responsible. No fault of Norma's that her Daddy was rich. Nonetheless, the pair of them had wronged me, to say nothing of poor Fred. I knew I'd forgive Gerald everything if he tied one of my braids around his wrist like he used to, and whispered, 'Madame, I am your prisoner!' But how could he do that if Norma was hanging around? I hardened my heart. She would have to go.

I began to recite the curse. 'Kazim magazim,' I chanted experimentally. 'Cymryd fy nghalon.' Then I submerged my body till only my face was out of water in order to give the words power. 'Take this heart, make it blacker than coal, swift as a swallow, more sour than the bitter salt sea . . .'

When the room was spinning with chant and my fingers were turning pruney, I emerged from the bath and sprinkled myself with lavender. In the sitting room Fred was slumped in front of the telly, wearing his best nylon balloon trousers. His head was drawn back into his body like a turtle and he was twisting the corner of his T-shirt into a ball.

'Why don't you go out and watch for your Dad?' I asked.

'Na, Mam,' he shrugged. 'You go.' So I did.

It had rained during the night but the morning was fresh and sunbeams danced on the jagged slate of Cwm Hyfryd quarry. In the garden the grass was lush and green. I prowled from the clothesline to the path at the top of the garden, mumbling my spell.

In the late afternoon, they arrived in a teal-blue Hertz rent-a-car with the roof-rack piled with luggage. I was checking the potato pie in the oven but something made me glance out the window: there was Norma, in thigh-high leather boots, mincing down the muddy path. She was wearing a leopard skin coat and a jaunty little pillbox hat that drew attention from her rather large nose. Behind her came Gerald in black mud-splattered leather, looking very unhappy.

I never expected a wave of pity to sweep over me as Norma stepped across our threshold. But her air of vulnerability make me realise she was just another poor girl, fallen prey to Gerald's exotic behaviour. Still, I could not allow compassion to cloud the issue.

'Please sit down,' I said. Norma removed her coat to reveal a black T-shirt with PARIS emblazoned in golden letters. She perched on the edge of a chair and began to drum softly on the table with enormous gold-lacquered fingernails. Then Fred sidled shyly into the room and froze in his tracks, gawking.

'This is Fred, Gerald,' I said. 'Look how he's grown!'

Gerald crossed the room and patted Fred's shoulder awkwardly, 'How are ya, son?'

Fred stared at the floor. The two of them stood motionless. Identical black hair. Same slanty eyes. 'He's the spitting image of you,' I said.

Norma must have felt very uncomfortable because she began to babble, 'We've got a stopover in Paris, France,' she said. 'You know that big hotel near the picture gallery, what's it called Gerald?' But Gerald said not a word. 'Everyone says the food in England's lousy,' she continued. 'But we had a three-course lunch on the way here – the prawn cocktail wasn't so bad, was it honey?'

I ignored her and served dinner. Norma didn't eat a thing but Gerald devoured my potato pie like a polecat. When he'd finished, I turned to Fred and said, 'Why don't you take your dad for a little walk up to the quarry? The rain's gone off now. Norma can stay here and look at your baby photos. If she likes.'

Well, I didn't for a moment think Norma would like. I knew she was dying to get out of my house and I was glad to see the back of her as well. After they went, I did the washing up and then I sat down by the open window. It was a glorious evening. The sky was powder blue and the sun lay like a sleeping cat across the kitchen table. An immense contentment crept over me. I was in control.

I could see them in my mind's eye, Fred and Gerald and Norma, threading their way up the steep path, the azure lake glinting in the quarry pit far below. I felt them climbing the stairway of giant slate slabs worn smooth by generations of footsteps; then they clambered across the scree, up to the marshy fringe of the abyss. I saw Gerald's fine features flushed with exhilaration, and Fred proudly pointing out the shadow of Ireland on the distant horizon, Norma's dark hair drifting back from her face as she teetered on the edge. And, in my mind, ever so gently, I toppled her into the quarry.

But my reverie was shattered by Fred's shrill cry. 'Mam! Mam! Come quick!' I flung open the door and raced to the mountain gate. Far above me, I could see Fred, leaping from rock to rock, his anorak flapping like a wounded heron. Behind him was a figure more difficult to discern, camouflaged against the gorse-blossoming hillside, loping and stumbling along. As it came nearer, I recognised with horror the black-sheathed thighs, the dappled crown. It was Norma.

Dear God, I gasped.

*

It might interest you to know, however, that now the inquest is over and the first floods of grief have subsided, I am coming to appreciate Norma's housekeeping skills and organising ability. We couldn't have managed the funeral without her. I'm afraid she is rather subdued these days –

she's even trimmed her fingernails. I suppose she must feel a bit isolated here without a driving licence but, fair play, she never complains.

We have spread her leopard coat beneath the shelf which holds the urn containing Gerald's ashes. An exotic touch, I thought, but not too ostentatious. The Hertz rent-a-car is still outside the door but I expect they'll reclaim it soon. These days Fred comes home to the two of us, peeling potatoes, buttering toast.

It's almost like being a family.

HOME TOWN

~

Nia Williams

There's a bench outside the Post Office. I sit there Saturday afternoons, after finishing the weekly shop and dragging up the hill, and have a quick fag before getting the bus. I'm down to three a day now: one first thing, one in the dinner break and one after tea. But Saturdays I put off the middle one: I have it outside, on the bench. All weathers.

So here I am. Cringeing into my coat, battered by the wind, watching the hamburger boxes and mangled Coke tins skim along the square. I'm trying to remember what used to be on the corner, where the Iceland is now. Some girl comes legging up the road – can't be more than 17 – shivering in a skinny-rib jumper and a tiny skirt. She avoids my eye and squeezes into the far corner of the seat. Sullen girl – but pretty. Slanting, feline eyes. She's leaning forward against the cold, tugging at the skirt's hem, knees clamped together. A torn trail of smoke escapes and drifts towards her: she gives it that look. I try and breathe in the opposite direction.

At her age we all smoked like chimneys. We used to hang out here, round this bench, me and the girls. Cackling over a packet of fags. Staring out the dirty looks. Oh, they used to look daggers at us, like we'd landed from Mars. Those round, thick-legged women in navy-blue macks, waddling past with their big canvas shopping bags. Always had bandages shimmering through their tea-coloured tights. We never realised how scared they were. Catrin Emmanuel would yell after them, 'Wassamatta love? We cramping your style?'

She had some mouth on her, Catrin, even then. I thought she was the bee's knees. Tall and thin and blonde, little eyes darting between wedges of mascara. She'd come swaggering across that square like she was really going places. But we only ever came to this bench.

Anyway. Best be off. I drop the butt end and grind it into the kerb. I can feel that girl's contempt drilling into the back of my head, so I gather my energy, find my balance and heave myself to my feet. Bend down to lift my three bulging carrier bags, and release a slight fart. The girl has turned away, cowering in the cold. Maybe she didn't notice.

Round the back of the library and past the stern Victorian huddle: Magistrates' Court, Social Services, Town Hall. Up Jubilee Street, past the bookies and the lawnmowers-and-parts shop. Tom Lloyd at the door, as usual, gazing mournfully at the scattering of passers-by. This was always a dead street, too far from the square and its welcoming names: Woolies, Smiths, Dorothy Perkins, Boots. It's even worse, now, since the Safeway opened on the ringway. Stan Jones the Butcher, with a half-empty counter. Hair Today – my mum went on calling it Sonia's Salon for years, even when Sonia was going doolally in a nursing home. There's a woman beaming from the poster, surrounded by curls that are fading at the edges; and a vase of dried flowers behind the grimy nets. I lumber round the corner to Station Road, where the shops peter out altogether. Just a row of blackened houses here, some of them boarded up, and the Queen's Arms, with its big new banner – 'Friday nite is Ladies nite'.

I know she's there before I see her. Before I turn past the last house and the street opens out. As soon as the first blue-and-yellow bus shelters appear I can smell her scent – heavy, treacly stuff, mingled with stale cigarettes. But maybe that's just my imagination.

Sure enough, though, there she is, leaning against the shelter's shallow bum-rest, shifting her legs to brace herself and avoid a trickle of old piss. Not bad, those legs, even now.

I'm trying to slow my pace. She hasn't looked round, but she knows I'm there. She takes a long, concentrated draw at her fag, opens her mouth to let the smoke cloud out and says 'Oright then?' without moving her head. I let my bags thud on to the ground.

'Going to work, are you?' I say. Got to say something. She sort of tuts and nods, and says, 'Late shift. Bastards.'

Catrin used to work in Tannyer and Sons, the fruit-and-veg shop in town. Then she moved to the new Safeway. She'd been at Tannyer's since school. I remember the way she announced it, with that throwaway voice. We'd all met up on the bench as usual, glowing with adult importance. Frances Key – already pregnant and fixing to marry Terry. Gaynor Foyle – going to Tech to do catering. I had a job lined up at the Town Hall. Filing and Admin, with the promise of secretarial training.

Catrin gave that little secretive, unsmiling laugh. We pressed round her, waiting, knowing: Catrin Emmanuel had a future. Not just days following days but a different kind – the kind we all felt tingling in our veins like fear. 'I'm all right,' she said. 'I'm going to Tanny's to sort out the Sons.'

And we grinned and cawed and whooped as if she'd said she was off to Hollywood.

Her hair's dyed now. Used to be creamy, silvery, gradually emerging like moonlight from the darker shadows around her head. Now it's sickly yellow and the roots need touching up.

She's kissing out the last of her fag and she says, 'Yeh, on till ten tonight. Still, beats watching Joe fiddle with himself in front of the telly.'

Joe was the second Tanny son. Catrin could have had her pick – could have had the shop and been opening two more branches by now. But the eldest boy, Robert, was ponderous and shy. Joe had thick black hair and wicked eyes and a reckless cornet-blast laugh.

I can tell she's uncomfortable. Busies herself putting out the fag against the shelter wall. 'Give me them old concrete shelters back any day,' she says. 'Put your stub out here, you're scared you'll melt the bugger.'

We both glare at the road where it disappears behind the railway station. Willing her bus to come.

The silence is stretching thin, and she seems to settle into another mood. I recognise it, in the detached, knowing half-smile. 'So,' she says. 'Been to get a video?'

She waits, tilting her face to judge my response. She's testing me. I can feel the heat creeping up my neck. I shift my eyes and start babbling, 'Just nipped in for Jake's film. You know. Nearly got him the new one with Mel Craig in, just to wind him up. In the end I got *The Usual Suspects*, that's more his kind of thing . . .'

Her face has sagged with scorn. I've distracted her with the mention of Mel Craig. Melanie Craig, she was, when we were at school. Never one of our lot. Always stood apart. Always seemed to be moving in another, luminous life. Took all the lead parts in the school dramas. Won prizes. Catrin called her Arty-arse, or Arty-tart. Or if that failed to get a laugh, Pigeon-tits. Not that it touched Melanie. She'd set her course. I picture it sometimes – Melanie Craig's great escape: on the train to London, watching the paper mill and the dishwasher factory and the wasteground all parading into her past. 'Have you seen the *state* of her?' Catrin explodes. 'Like a fucking Christmas tree, all glitter and bangles.'

'I've never seen her films,' I say, and regret the plea in my voice.

'All crackheads and tarts, it is. Making people look dense and dirty – it's not right. And *her*, swanking about like Miss Had-em-All – *her*, Frigid Freda, who never had more than one arsehole in her knickers that *I* knew . . .' Finally, Catrin's bus comes jolting round the bend. She waves and winks at the driver and the door opens with a sigh.

'S'long then,' she blares over her shoulder, and I can relax.

It's getting on for closing time now, but I'm first in my bus queue, so I get the best seat – upstairs, over the driver. I put my bags on the seat next to me, even though people are standing in the aisle and making pointed comments. I need a bit of room to spread, these days.

It's a funny thing, how inside the bus it's all rock-hard chewing gum under the seats, and Twix wrappers and apple cores on the floor, and Delyth Watts Is A Slag in thick black felt pen under the window, and the stink of cheese-and-onion crisps and damp jumpers. But you see the other buses passing, on a winter afternoon, and they always look so comforting, with every face framed in a square of light, and the engines rumbling, rising and falling, like Grandad used to sound with his poor old chest. When we reach the top of Juniper Hill, partly to take my mind off the sarky comments ('I hope she's paid for two seats'), I wrestle Jake's video out of the bag. The cover shows a row of men in an identity parade or something, all looking like they couldn't give a toss. Most of them will come to a sticky end, that's for sure – that's the kind of film Jake likes. Action. *Reservoir Dogs* – one of his favourites. Anything with explosions. He loves them. Though you'd never guess it, seeing him slung on to the sofa with his face all blank.

The new boy served me at the video hire. Spots on his forehead and a stud in his nose, poor dab. It's not that I was avoiding Harry. Just that the young lad was free. Harry tends to do the backroom stuff these days.

Personally I don't go for the guns-and-grenades type films. Jake says I live in Cloud-Cuckoo Land, but I don't care. I prefer a good old-fashioned whodunnit. Ruth Rendell, Inspector Morse, *Murder at the Vicarage* – that sort of thing. Something where it's all sorted out at the end. 'It's not real, is it?' says Jake. 'Life's not like that.' He can say what he likes. If what he watches is real life, he can keep it.

Of course, it's a battle to get off the bus – nobody's going to shift for me to get past, after I hogged the best seat. So I have to bellow down the stairs for the driver to wait. Embarrassing. I bet Melanie Craig doesn't have to do all this, I think, as I'm staggering off the step. I bet she's got a limo and a chauffeur in a cap. Or at least takes a taxi. As the bus starts up again a toddler smears its snotty hand down the window.

I did bring back a Mel Craig film once. Just to see. Didn't appeal to me, though. No story. One scene looked like one of the empty steelworks a few miles from here. Melanie and some bloke, in a kind of dingy, dripping shed, all girders and broken glass. And they start clawing each other, tugging each other's shirts off, and then they're at it on the floor – on that floor! In all the puddles and grit and God knows what. I had to fast forward. Well, I've never liked sex scenes. Never met a soul who does. Anything like that comes on, and we start laughing, or we go quiet, or Jake goes off to get a beer. Thing is, it doesn't even turn you on, does it? Now – Sergeant Lewis, and his accent – that's sexy. Or David Attenborough, getting all agitated about a kiwi. Or even Alan Titchmarsh, if I'm in the mood. But I don't want them taking so much as their socks off, thanks very much.

'Got my tape?' he calls, before I'm through the door. He's in there watching the results with the curtains closed.

'Yes,' I say, 'but *you'll* have to take it back, OK?'

I've got a million and one things to do.

I never told Jake about Harry. He wouldn't be very interested. Probably say Catrin's a silly bitch and leave it at that. He's never taken to her. And then of course there are other things he might say. Maybe that's why I haven't told him.

He calls the video hire Harry the Pak's. Doesn't mean anything – that's what everyone calls it. Even to Harry's face. Harry just smiles. Even when the kids copy his accent. He just smiles. Or he used to.

I can hear that voice on the telly, reading out the results, going up-and-up; up-and-down. Sometimes it's quite comforting, but today it's driving me nuts. I'm in the kitchen, unpacking the shopping. I could shut the door, but I want the contact. This stark light in here makes the window pitch black. I love having a garden. But I have these dreams, about people moving in the bushes at night. It's not the people who scare me – it's the fact that nothing I do can clear away the darkness.

When I've done I pull the blind down and go upstairs to sit in the spare room. This room is always all right, even in the dark. In fact, I haven't bothered to switch the light on. This was Kelly's room, and this is where she thinks we should put a computer, instead. She's got it into her head that we're really going to buy one. Says *everyone* will have one before long, just like the phone and the telly. She's probably right – she's a bright girl. Could have stayed on in school, but she was out and over to the Tech as soon as it was legal. Couldn't stick this town a minute longer, she said. This hole. Got herself a room with three other girls, near the college. Well, they're nice girls, two of them went to school with her. They all think they're seeing the world. But it's only two stops on the train.

'Get yourself fixed up, Mum,' she says, 'and you can nag me about what I eat on the e-mail instead of on the phone.'

'Yes,' I said, 'and I know what that means – it means there'll be nobody there to listen.'

'Oh *Mum*,' she said, in that way they've got. '*Everyone* can listen if you're on the net. You can reach the whole *world* without leaving the house.'

'Well in that case,' I said, 'you might as well come and live back here with us.'

That shut her up.

I don't know what Kelly would say about this Harry business. She might wonder what all the fuss is about. I mean, maybe she'd be right. Why am I so bothered? It was something of nothing. So why am I always up here, in the half-light, churning it over in my head?

I wasn't even planning to go into the video hire that day. Jake had borrowed some western off a mate. I was in Woolies, and I saw Catrin choosing a CD for her niece's birthday. We were having a laugh – she was threatening to buy *Best of the Tremeloes* from the cut-price rack, 'show her what a bloody good tune is like.' I was saying how my mother used to make me listen to Matt Munro. We left Woolies together and she said, 'Hang on, I want a word with *him*,' and opened the door into Harry's shop. She turned to me and said, 'Look at him, grinning like a bloody hyena.' I was already smiling back at Harry, but I gave her a sly look. Well, that's how she is. All mouth.

Up she went to the counter, clack-clack-clack in her heels, and started going on about some tape Joe had hired. Harry was saying something about a fixed fine, and pointing past her at a notice about late returns. 'It's the rules,' he kept saying. She wanted the money back. She was jabbing her finger into the air. Harry kept pointing at this poster.

'It's the rules.'

And then her voice changed.

I only ever heard it go that way a couple of times before: when some girl nicked her boyfriend in the fourth year; and once when the English teacher told her to put her chest away and clam up. She stood up in the class, the desk scraped forward, and she began a sort of screech. Made me think of rooks. She had to clean the school loos for a week.

'Don't give me it's the fucking rules.'

I stood at the back of the shop and watched her shoulders lift and spread into black, ragged wings. Her words rasped against her throat. 'Give us our money back and fuck off home, you thieving Paki bastard.' For a split second we all froze. Then, like a child who's gone too far, she went further. A long wing swung forward. There was a muffled clap, a clattering, and a terrible, sick plunge in my stomach.

Catrin turned sharply, examining her hand. She'd struck him clumsily, splitting a nail and leaving a small crescent of blood on his cheek. Harry bent down to scrabble for his glasses. I stepped forward, made a weak mime of helping him pick them up.

Catrin had clicked past me and she stood waiting, holding the door. Well, Harry had found his glasses. There was nothing for me to do. I followed her out.

We walked in silence across the square, then she said she was going to get Joe his paper. She said 'S'long then,' and left me standing by the bench.

I watched her striding away. Quick, long steps. I always used to wish I could walk like Catrin.

The sport's finished and Jake is yelling about tea. I'm sitting here, in Kelly's room, and I'm shaking.

I get up and look at the silhouette in the mirror. I used to pretend I was Catrin – in the bathroom, at home, I used to repeat the things she said, mouth them at my reflection, and flick back imaginary moonbeam hair. I don't say I *liked* her. Shouldn't think she likes me, particularly. That's not the point. It's like everything else – the house, the new computer, this town – love and hate doesn't come into it. It's just the way things are.

So it doesn't make sense that I keep raking over and over the whole thing. Life goes on. It's all settled down again. It doesn't make sense for me to feel so churned up. Or to keep wishing Harry the Pak had never come to our town.

OWL

~

Susan Morgan

There was no shape on Sarah. She was this snobby girl with braces who'd come up the farm, all the way from Swansea. Did she want to have fun? No, she did what she was told, nice and tidy. She even agreed to bath and baby-sit the two Budd brats so that Mr and Mrs Budd could go down the pub one evening. Megan wouldn't dream of doing such a thing. She was going down the White Horse herself, under age. She didn't give a damn.

Megan came from the village near the farm, but was sleeping over because they had to be up so early, catching the ponies and getting them fed, groomed and tacked-up for the pony-trekkers. She was strong-willed and well developed for fifteen. Sarah saw this and was envious, knowing she could never be like her.

It was the same with Gull. This was a pony that had run off, a little grey mare Mr Budd sighted the day they led a group of Brownies pony-trekking up the Vole to the River Twrch. He told them Gull had been missing since early June. That evening he drove his battered car as far as the filter beds at the waterworks, where the road ended. Then he made them walk up on to the mountain, coming across the pony almost straight away.

'Remember, horses always try to run uphill,' he warned, positioning them for a chase, armed with sticks and ropes as if they were out to capture something wild.

'Let me have a go first,' said Gaynor Budd. Shaking a bowl

of knobbies, she called Gull and it wasn't long before the little grey was placidly plodding homewards, away from her few months of freedom on the mountain with two wild mares and their foals. The next day she was back at work, carrying a young girl up the trail to Llyn-y-fan Fawr. She was like Sarah, happy to please.

Finding Gull coincided with the onset of a fine spell of weather. The first week the skies had been leaden and Sarah imagined Megan was a witch, whipping up the wind on purpose so that it hurled icy drops of rain right through her, placing rocks on the track to trip her up and gorse bushes to catch and scratch her. But the morning after Gull's return the clouds lifted, the skies lightened and the hills prepared to lay back in a summery haze. As she plodded up the trail following the fat rump of the pony in front, Sarah watched Megan gradually strip off till she wore nothing but bra and shorts. The little girl riding Gull giggled and looked impressed.

When they got to Llyn-y-fan Fawr Sarah studiously noted that it was a natural corrie lake, the larger of two. Apart from that, there was nothing there, just grass and water, mountain and sky. The moors rolled away on black peaty soil, scattered with rocky outcrops like broken teeth and the mountain reared back in a great cliff, raw and scarred where earth had slipped. The sky seemed emptied, looking down impassively on the little lake, with its lapping waves and tiny sandy beach, where no one sunbathed.

Snobby Sarah would never have fun, Megan thought. It was boiling, a boiling hot day, and they were all red in the face and sweating like pigs, especially her and Sarah, because they were doing the bloody leg work. The spoilt brat Brownies just sat there like sacks of potatoes and complained. The lake looked lovely, really lovely, refreshing, just right to cool off in. Megan was so thirsty she felt she'd like to gorge on it.

'Going in for a swim?'

'I've not brought bathers.'

'Who wants bathers? Wear bra and knickers.'

Sarah couldn't. Just as she never smiled, because she wore a brace on her teeth. She felt the same about her body. There were things you had to hide. Still, she paddled, feeling the bottom of the lake, which was springy and soft, like a sponge. When she scrunched up her toes in the peat, little clouds of rusty brown unfurled in the icy water to hang around her ankles.

'Yee-ha!' yelled Megan, squealing as she let herself fall back in the water, screeching as the cold hit her. Her screams reverberated against the mountain cliff.

'I'm such a TWAT!' she shouted, splashing about and pretending to drown, her strong brown legs waving in the air. Some of the ponies raised their heads at the commotion.

Every day the sun bore down on them as they led the ponies with nervous riders to different destinations, across expanses of sun-bleached moorland, with cotton-grass, heather and gorse. They looked forward to their evenings off and usually went up the lane to the Water Board house where a boy called Howard lived, with his parents. Near his house he had dammed the river to make a pool for skimming stones and some nights they lit a fire there and tried to bake potatoes.

His mam and dad spoilt it all one night, coming down the pool to see what he was up to, Mam with her lined face all screwed up with worry for her only baby son. His dad, well, if the truth be known, Megan thought he fancied her, the way he tried to be hip, with Howie's guitar, singing bloody 'Country Roads' and offering them beers. It turned her stomach, an old man trying to be hip. They spoilt it, coming down the pool, so the next night she asked Howard did he want to go up the waterfall.

Megan showed them the way, up the side of a stream, armed with a bottle of cider. She walked ahead with Howard and Sarah scrambled after them, trying to eavesdrop, even though they hardly spoke. The path petered out and the stream became a torrent, so that they were forced to scramble up slippery banks till they saw, below them in a gully, water sliding glassily over a ledge, into a pool that looked deep and ominously dark.

'Who's for a skinny dip?' yelled Megan, already undoing the belt on her jeans.

She has no shame, Sarah thought, watching her strip off in front of Howard, who turned away, as if overcome. She plunged into the pool with screams that could be heard down the Swansea Valley, and spat out water in a spray, standing for a moment like the statue of a goddess, her breasts translucent in the dying light.

'Come on in, it's lovely!'

He did join her and Sarah began to undress, folding her clothes, watching the two of them. Howard walked in till he was waist deep and stood there, white and gaunt, his thin shoulders shaking with the cold. Megan splashed him and dived to tickle him under the water and he laughed and groaned, before falling in after her.

As Sarah picked her way across slippery rocks to climb in she thought it a magical place, a moss-carpeted hollow, overhung by slender berry-strung rowan branches and luxurious ferns, but dangerous too, like a wound welling up. There was the ache from the ice-cold water to contend with, and an ache inside, because Megan was with Howard.

She slipped into the water and felt the breath knocked out

of her by the shock of the cold. She had to tread water for a while, gasping, and then found herself enjoying it, the splashing and fooling about, and making a racket.

The three of them sat afterwards huddled together, their bodies shaken by violent shudders as they tried to pull on clothes over limbs that had gone numb and wouldn't get dry. Then they swigged from the cider bottle in turns and Sarah felt her face slipping and her head begin to spin. She couldn't help herself when she started to laugh as Howard failed to tie up the laces on his pumps because of his trembling fingers and she bent over to do them for him and forgot not to smile.

'Come back to my house to warm up,' he stuttered, and they half-ran, half-fell down the mountainside. It was quite dark when they got to the strange modern kitchen and even Megan was tongue-tied and shy under bright fluorescent lights. Howard's mother scolded them for being so daft and made them drink hot chocolate before shooing the two girls back off to the farm.

Sarah felt her skin tingling all over as she and Megan ran gleefully down the lane, frightening each other in the pitch-blackness when a night bird screeched close by.

The last day before she was to go back to Swansea, Mr Budd asked Sarah to ride Owl, a white colt he had been schooling on a long rein in the yard.

She had to move slowly around him and lean on his smooth bare back before Mr Budd gently saddled him and helped her mount. Neither of them spoke and everything went in slow-motion, except for Owl, who was jumpy and alert, his ears pricked forward towards any sound. She rode him first around and around the yard on the long rein till Mr B said to try him up the lane as far as the gate to the mountain.

Sarah liked him, his small neat body moving beneath her,

and as the late afternoon sun warmed her back and shoulders, she felt she could almost close her eyes and let the clopping sound of his hooves lull her to sleep. A robin sang brilliantly from the hedgerow and she loosed the reins and let the pony pick at morsels from the side. It was the first time she had ridden completely alone and the thought they could go anywhere scared and excited her.

At the rickety old gate to the mountain she leaned forward to see if she could see the Water Board house and Howard, but there was no sign of life. She hoped Megan had not gone there and persuaded him to listen to records in his room.

The little pony put his head over the gate and breathed in deeply, as if scenting the mountain. She thought if she opened the gate and let him go, he would be away, bucking and kicking at the memory of being tethered and controlled. She turned him back towards the farm and into the sun, urging him into a trot and then a canter.

When she got back to the yard, Mrs Budd was sitting on the low garden wall, looking out for her. She came over to help her dismount and lead the pony to the stable shed.

'You did really well,' she said, 'I'm impressed. That's the first time Owl's been ridden.'

Sarah was surprised how calm she felt. Perhaps it was because she hadn't built it up beforehand in her mind. They brushed him down and Sarah loved the satisfying rhythmic crunch as he ate from a bucket. She felt very happy.

'I wanted you to ride him,' said Gaynor, 'because you've got a light touch.'

Sarah nodded. She thought she knew what Gaynor meant.

'You've missed Megan. She's gone off home, said she wanted to get ready for a big night out, now she's got her wages. She works hard and plays hard, does our Megan. Oh, and Howard called for you, on the phone, said to meet him later by the pool? Wants to say good-bye.'

Hoping Gaynor would think the flush on her face was sunburn, smarting in the setting sun, Sarah looked at her nervously. Mrs Budd caught her round the waist and gave her an encouraging squeeze.

'You should go for it, Sarah, love. Wicked to shrink and shy away, not show what you're made of!'

A TASTE OF THINGS TO COME

~

Rachel Sayer

The tomatoes felt soft, so soft and round and plump in the palms of my hands, and the mushrooms through which I sliced so easily fell into a delicate temper of a sauce. I do admit for a minute there I thought the onions might make me cry but I remedied that thought straight away with a drop or two of passionate red wine.

I could practically feel the tingling in my loins, excitement slowly creeping down my spine as I let the cheese walk quietly in musty smells over the red grapes. They seemed somehow, the grapes, to pout at me. I remember quite vividly those cherry lips that whispered urgent messages of support.

'Don't give up now, something beautiful is about to be made.'

So I consulted the book once again. Decades and histories it had lain in our family, written in a Welsh that made me feel I was chewing cobwebs as I read. Whenever you were sad or just bad and needed changing I always consulted the book. You used to laugh at me. No matter what it was though, or who it was, it always brought you back, didn't it?

I had just finished the perfect blend of aroma and taste that had a character and personality all of its own when you walked in. You used your old set of keys in that easy arrogant manner of yours.

You can leave those behind you tonight, I thought.

It was a good job I had already dressed myself in my soft cashmere black dress. Already curled my hair in soft halos around my head. Already fed the cat. Now she just sat lazily in black, curled on the cream sofa. Reflections of me and the preparations in her green eyes.

Friendly peck on the cheek and a perfunctory bottle of wine. Did you hold me a little too closely for a little too long a time?

You didn't forget the bar of chocolate though. It was a delight watching you melt the chunks into liquid, molten velvet while the flames from my old Welsh stove cast a pink red glow on your exquisite features. I thought, You'll do.

And the cat prowling your newly-shone shoes as if she were hungry for food.

Later, as the champagne teased my tongue, I wondered if it was having the same effect on you. The first twenty minutes were a strain on my nerves, you see. That is until I saw the first oyster slip down your throat in one gentle and easy movement.

While the green-eyed monster just watched now, from the opposite side of the room.

'Delicious,' you said as you closed your eyes to savour the moment.

Just keep them closed for a while longer, I prayed.

What I actually said was, 'Welsh. Welsh oysters, fresh from Conwy.'

And to follow we ate in a familiar comfort the pleasure of slow-baked leek souffle and local gooseberry wine to compliment the taste. I remember hoping that you were not too full. I suppose it was a leftover from the painful days of cooking for you while you ate then fell asleep. Quickly I erased that memory. I just needed you energetic for one night. Just a couple of hours. You could sleep forever after that for all I cared. You wore a red polo-neck that harshly set off the severity of your jawline. Snugly-fitting jeans that seemed to say, 'Come and join us in the adoration of this body that makes us look so good.'

You looked crueler than I remembered. Harder somehow. Still . . . hauntingly beautiful.

'I must admit, I'm surprised at how grown up you are being about the whole situation,' you said.

'Me too,' I murmured through mouthfuls of exquisite tastes.

The chocolate over the strawberries was nothing short of perfect but it was the little edible petals that you couldn't get over. You talked all evening of how much happier you were. How you had despised my love for home-making.

How all along you had always wanted a career girl with no desires for a family or anything as suffocating.

'If I'm honest,' you said, which I thought was slightly ironic, 'it was your cooking that kept me with you for so long. Ten long years for the love of food. I must have been mad. You should make the most of what you've got. Open a restaurant that specialises in Welsh food perhaps. I'd definitely come.'

I know you would, I thought.

A little bit of cheese. Not too much, but just enough to satisfy a delicate sufficiency. The clock struck midnight and the timing and the temperature were exactly right.

The wind was howling across my Motherland and it poured harshly and heavily into the sturdy little windows of my cottage. I said a silent prayer of 'thank you' for this. My cosy living room with its blaring log fire, cream sofa, thick rugs and stone floor. Cocooning . . . like a womb. Warm.

That's when you made love to me – here on this sofa. Slowly and sweetly until torrents of us came crashing on to our bodies.

In the aftermath, I took one last look at you. A beautiful

wet, well-defined man. Exactly what I needed. Arrogance and confidence personified.

Then the rain stopped.

I told you it was time you left before she wondered where you were. I half-pushed you out of the door, eager as I was to be rid of you. Eager as I was to be left alone with the dark bitter sweet brandy. My last for some time.

You even sent me a card after that night. An afterthought.

'Thank you for the wonderful food. I'm so glad we can be friends and I'm so relieved that after ten years you don't hold it against me that I didn't want to have children with you. Nothing personal. I'm a free spirit which I know that you now understand. Perhaps you could look upon the kitten I bought you ten years ago as a substitute family. I just can't do that kind of commitment, you know. Scares the hell out of me. Besides I've got better things to spend my money on. I especially enjoyed your goodbye gift though. Be a good girl and let's just keep it between ourselves OK.'

Now my belly feels soft, so soft and round and full in the palms of my hands.

Funny, how when I sent you my reply which contained the letter from the child support agency, you sounded like you were about to have kittens, not a beautiful little son.

FEATHERS

~

Kaite O'Reilly

Her name was Mary Bangs and she walked like a chicken. All her clothes she wore at once, bags getting in the way of her crooked wings of arms. Every day throughout that summer she pecked along the high street, sharp chin jutting, crooning her little bird song. All of us children were afraid of her, but to our parents she was a figure of fun – 'You're a right Mary Bangs' if our combination of clothing fell short of their approval. She looked like a charity aid parcel bursting through its string. At night she slept in a shop doorway, head under elbow, like a hen on her perch.

That was the summer we were held to siege. Breasts budded and voices cracked under the strain of violence inflicted on our bodies. Med and Dai stopped speaking, resigning themselves to grunts or surly shakes of the head. Their soft voices were no longer their own, betraying them in squeaks or a booming resonance. White fluff appeared on their chins, like the soft down on the small of our backs we used to tickle, in gentler games. Strange hair began to sprout elsewhere and we stopped our gymnastic rough and tumble, carrying our elastic limbs sullenly.

It was bewildering, we were shameful. We hated our parents for not warning us of this catastrophe and wanted to kill them for their indulgent jokes about our bean-pole size. All grown-ups were conspirators, for someone could have told us We loathed them equally and with a vengence, except for Mary Bangs. She was exempt for the simple reason she wasn't an adult. Mary Bangs was a chicken and spoke in clucks.

She would crow and chirrup and croon along the embankment where we lay on burnt grass, plotting revenge on our elders. The river seemed stagnant, thick with chemicals, and no one came to fish, having given up that pretence years ago.

Sometimes the brewery burped out its hop stench and we could tell what day it was by the artificial flavourings creeping out from the bakery. Vanilla was Monday, burnt chocolate on biscuits smelt Friday. We lay sandwiched between the brewers and bakers, saying all we needed was a candlestick maker.

A butcher we had, Four Fingered Malachy, who lived under the bridge on a pile of carpet samples. He would join us sometimes, letting us touch his butchered fingers, skin still pink and blind like baby mice.

They reminded me of cropped terrier's tails, the knobbled digits sticking upright, blunted, sore. An Uncle in Ireland de-tailed a litter of Jack Russells once, offering me the dismembered bones hidden in his closed hand, as a treat. It was a child's game we played, suddenly nightmarish as I took the load, expecting sweets. A palm full of puppy dog's tails, the bones startlingly white within the wiry case.

It was the first act of cruelty I had suffered from an adult and I felt my stomach tip watching Malachy roll cigarettes with his spoiled hands. As he raised the butt to his mouth I remembered my Uncle's laugh and wanted to be sick.

I never showed it if I wanted to retch, for that would signal my inferiority, being the only member of the gang who was a girl. It was a biological fact which had been invisible until that summer. Previously, it was easy to ignore with our twig-like limbs and squirming bodies. I wore my hair short like theirs and never suffered from the girlish fears which made us contemptuous of many in our class. I could jump as high and run as fast as the best of them and learnt how to pee standing up, surreptitiously wiping myself dry with grass afterwards. I was a girl with the simple ambition of wanting to grow up a boy. Then my body denounced me with its bizarre mutations. Med and Dai looked at me with the same horror with which I had greeted their own developments. We knew in our hearts it was the last summer we would play together and even then I think we mourned the loss of innocence.

For it was not just our bodies which were changing. The world was losing its shine, the comforting routine which spun about us as the central cogs, now creaked and threatened to change its pattern. Our mothers stopped calling for us until they were hoarse at the garden gate come dusk. This was a particularly satisfying battle of nerves where we timed our resistance to their growing hysteria until the emotional umbilical cord snapped us back to their sides. Whether we would get a beating or not added an extra frisson to the exercise and we hunkered in the dark, waiting their call.

When they failed to come, we trailed in, distraught, finding them easy at the kitchen table and not laid out, victim to some dreaded accident, as we feared. Our references to missing our bedtime were met with indolent 'oh really?'s and the lack of supper with, 'Surely you're big enough to get that yourself, now?' Stung, we stood wreathed in curls of their cigarette smoke, as unnoticed as the smears of lipstick on the china cups which dangled precariously from their fingers.

The place we'd inhabited before was run smoothly as a little ship, everything in its right place and order, parents the stewards to our every whim. Suddenly we saw we were in dangerous waters, the ship was keeling to the side and the crew were lethargic mutineers who didn't seem to like us much. Their words said one thing whilst their lips shaped another. Their eyes had a dull film over them, like the moment in the pictures when you haven't been told but you just know the loyal servant is really the murderer and now they're going to turn the axe on you.

In all this horror only Mary Bangs remained intact. The dart of her head held the same simplicity and her cautious mistrust echoed our own. She continued her unsullied clucking and pecking, and in our minds she became an accomplice, no longer a figure to haunt.

She stayed alone, unlike the other houseless people we saw who banded together to be raucous and safe from the people with houses. We never saw her lounging or singing against the Taff railings, beckoning us with fingers for a kiss or adult secret. She hobbled along, earthed in the soil. She looked happiest clucking over large pebbles stolen from the cobbled lane development in the docks, settling her skirts about them, preparing to roost.

We knew something terrible had happened to her, an experience which turned her brain from being human to birdlike. She was a tragic figure and the adults' refusal to see this, but to continue with barbed jokes at her expense, confirmed our belief: she was an outcast from the awful adult society. During the secret initiation ceremony she had rejected The Way, but the magnitude of what she had learned buckled and distorted her. Poor weak Mary Bangs, her brains mashed to jam.

We swore we, too, would refuse the fate our parents seemed to be preparing us for, but we had fortitiude and would not escape into chickenhood like our unfortunate comrade. We would stand firm and become daring outlaws, fulfilling the promise often yelled at our parents: 'I'm never going to be like you.'

Meanwhile, we felt like sacrificial lambs when meeting adults on the street. Their coded comments to our mothers about our size and sulky development hinted at the initiation to come. Some even rubbed their hands together in malicious glee, their long teeth yellow and pointed. 'Not long now, eh?' We ignored them, striking bored poses as we stared at a plane's solitary progress across the sky.

Just last summer we had been polite and sickeningly endearing to these crones, who patted our arms and slipped us small change when our mothers were supposed not to be looking. We knew now the pats were those of a meat dealer's at a cattle auction, checking our progress and encouraging our traitor bones to telescope out.

We'd been conned. Even though we recoiled from the contagion of adult behaviour, we reasoned we needed to know about it, the better to resist. Forewarned was after all, forearmed.

After a council of war we set out, trawling the backstreets and waterways for experience. We lingered in concrete corners in the city centre and scrubland next to municipal buildings where empty bottles or urine-soaked blankets littered the roots of unpruned bushes. They were lairs of unknown creatures, thrilling in speculation. Like detectives we scrutinised the scene of inquiry, but never close enough to touch or be touched by the adult squalor we sought with relish.

Previously, our unity was viewed as cute and cause for much smiling and aah-ing amongst our elders. Now, perhaps suspecting our vowed refusal of grown-updom, our intimacy was deemed unsavoury and 'not natural', with frowned adult glances at the goat's nubs rising on my front.

'Divide and rule' we had learnt from Dai's Socialist Grandpa, so we clung together, knowing we were weaker alone. We had such confidence in our camaraderie, when the first desertion came we merely blinked at it and grew silent, staring in mild interest at the amputation where Med used to be.

We would never know the torture he experienced, the subtle brain-washing or sensory deprivation which had loosened the link. He simply dropped from our company, leaving a clean scar like those on heavily pruned rose bushes, where a branch had once cleaved.

It happened on a Saturday, one of those golden days when we children want to be outside but grown-ups most definitely want to stay in. We'd always scorned the male habit of watching TV sport on a hot day when the sun cracked the soil and there were hours of running around to be had in the brewery air. We pitied the incompetents who sat cracking open beer in pop cans, growing pasty in the gloom, one curtain drawn as the rays bleached the picture on the TV set.

We were infinitely superior creatures who knew every inch of the *milltir sgwâr* – which bushes the cats crawled under to die and where sour grass and wild raspberries grew in the car exhaust fumes by the public baths. There were so many things to discover. Although we'd stretched our knowledge to include the by-ways of adults, it was an incredible thought to pass over adventures for sitting in a stuffy room, watching packs of adult males running around stupidly, chasing different sized balls. Yet that was exactly what Med wanted. To our disbelief he crouched down amongst his hairy, curry-belching brothers, eyes glued to the set, mumbling 'Naah, I think I'll stay in. S'alright, this.'

At first we guessed this was a particularly clever piece of scouting. Like the white man with forked tongue in Westerns, he'd infiltrated the enemy camp to gather intelligence and would shoot off before they realised his cunning in the second half. We were full of admiration for him, until he took a slug from the can his hairiest brother offered and a drag from the rolly another presented. At that moment we lost him. We knew the score. Once he'd smoked the pipe of peace, he was effectively in their tribe. The guffaws and pats on his back from his brothers when he fulfilled this rite even resembled the pow-wowing of the Indians in the *Different Cultures of the World* film we'd been shown in class.

Med's desertion struck us deeply and we knew we had to be extra-vigilant. The enemy could strike in the most unexpected places and as we'd never tested ourselves as individuals, who knew what our weaknesses might be.

The main flaw presented itself quickly – it was in our numbers. Two does not constitute a gang. Two is a pair. Two can be called 'a couple'.

Despite scowling whilst fingering rusty penknives and scratching my legs with brambles to prove my boyishness, in adult eyes our status had changed. From cadre and fellow outlaw, Dai suddenly became 'my boyfriend'. It was fatal; a charge from which he could never recover.

The rest of that summer was a lonely business. I tried to continue as before, tracing animal tracks in dried mud, or skimming stones across the oily skin of the river. I attempted, once, to laze on the embankment but Four Fingered Malachy joined me with an insistence which was unsettling. I left, shortly afterwards. He had a look in his eyes which was frightening, one I didn't want to learn to understand.

I heard that Med and Dai had teamed up again, with a tougher gang who hung round the amusement arcade. They were famous for terrorising cats and taunting the off-licence Alsation until it foamed at the mouth and had to be put down.

My parents quoted this as proof of a fortunate escape. Med

and Dai were of poor stock – 'bad blood will out' – my separation from their influence showed the low droop was not in me. I was uncomfortable with their superior congratulations. Unknown to them, I had met again with my former blood brothers the week before.

They were loitering by the egg stall in the outside market, sharing a cigarette with an older boy who was minding the pitch. We greeted each other coolly, in our insolent way, and fell back into the companionable silence which had been the signature of our latter days.

It was then we heard the familiar scratching and clucking. Mary Bangs, crook-winged, crowing and preening her way along the pavement.

Perhaps our youthfulness made her less wary, or a sense of our earlier empathy had slipped somehow into her birdlike brain. Either way, she approached us without suspicion, tilting her jaw curiously, stabbing the air as she softly crooned. It soon became clear we were not the subject of her attentions. She cooed at the pyramid of stacked calcium, tapped with tenderness at the brown and speckled shells.

When the first egg was thrown there was a delay before she registered the slug trail of mucus sliding down her face. The second broke on her collarbone, its yellow startling against her skin. As the fourth and fifth were hurled an unearthly noise rose from her throat; Med and Dai were laughing, smashing the eggs on the pavement. She tried to save them, hands slimy, pushing the yolks into useless shards. I was screaming, catching their wrists, willing them to stop now, stop, can't you see that she is crying. The older boy pushed me sideways, the adults were coming. Med put an egg in my hand and said now was the time, I had to do it to prove I was one of them. Mary Bangs scooped broken shell off the pavement. Dai spat, calling me chicken. I was a real girlie, wasn't I? A real girl. She opened her mouth, no bird sound came out, but a terrible keening. She looked at me as the egg left my hand. It was then I understood the nature of a maiming initiation. The air was suddenly silent, and rank with grief.

THE BLACKBERRY SEASON

~

Jo Hughes

It's said that no blackberries should be picked after the eighth of October because that's the day the devil tried to get into heaven. Old Gabriel was waiting at the gates and he wasn't a man to be easily fooled. He threw that old devil out. The devil went falling through the sky; down, down he went through the stratosphere and ionosphere, past snail clouds and cirrus clouds until, thump, he landed in a thorny black-berry bush. The devil got so angry he spat and spat and didn't stop spitting until the whole bush was covered with foamy phlegm. The berries turned mouldy and bitter, and ever since that time, each year on that day, they do the same.

So when Linda said that I ought to make some friendly gesture to Catherine to show that there were no hard feelings I decided that a home-baked pie might be just the thing. Blackberries, of course; it was the season. To make it extra special I decided to pick the fruit at night; midnight on the eighth.

I crept into the garden with my torch and my colander and prayed that no one would see me. The night was cold. A familiar crisp, frost smell met me and brought back memories of bonfires and fireworks. It was the smoky scent of October and November and December; those magic months of strange ritual. There was a night for witches and a night for burning effigies. There were days of angels and mistletoe and pine trees and a night of *Auld Lang Syne*. Now, in the garden, I would make my own bitter-sweet ritual as I picked the shining clusters of fruit.

The moon was full and silvery and I found the berries easily in its light. The colander was soon full and I laughed a little at myself as I carried it back through the nettles and brambles without a single sting or scratch. I had no belief in my sorcery, the whole business merely amused me. It was a happy revenge. I could have cooked her an apple pie and spat in it myself but the devil's spit was better. Besides, to spit in it myself was too low, too dirty, and too much what she'd expect of me.

This would be enough, this friendly gift baked with loving care. I thought about our meeting, how she'd hug me and say, 'Oh Susan, dear Susan, I'm so sorry things had to happen the way they did!' and all the time she'd be gloating inside like a cat that's killed a great, fat rat. She was the queen of control, she switched smiles and tears on and off like an actress in a long-running show; her eyes glistened and her teeth flashed in a smile, but the feelings had long ago been forgotten. She was a surgeon with emotions as finely honed as a scalpel and like a surgeon she knew just which one to choose at the appropriate moment. So, from caring concern she'd move to nostalgia: 'It's so sad, it was so good at the beginning. We were all so . . .' Then her lip would begin to tremble and she'd try very hard to smile. At this point I should, of course, also be on the brink of tears and I should hug her fluttering, sparrow shoulders and weep like a baby, but I won't. Instead I shall just say that it's all in the past now and what the hell and other such platitudes. Then, I will give her the pie.

The house was dark and silent when I entered, the hall lights had been switched off and everybody, I supposed, must be in bed. It was warm in the kitchen as I'd turned the oven on in preparation for my night's baking. I put on a tape of Wagner's 'The Ring' for a bit of company, then rinsed the fruit under the tap and thought some more about Catherine. I remembered how nice I had thought she was when we were first introduced: 'Susan, this is Catherine. Catherine, this is Susan.' I turned to find a small, blonde woman beaming at me, her hand outstretched towards me. We shook hands.

'I've heard so much about you. You must be very proud of the work you've done for the gallery. Jenny tells me it was you who arranged the "Man-made Images" exhibition. I thought that was marvellous, so pertinent to current feminist discourse and art theory.'

I smiled; I just liked the pictures. I also liked flattery.

I turned off the tap and found myself grinning at the blackberries and remembered that I had no reason to smile. I felt the old anger rise up like indigestible dough swelling inside the walls of my chest, choking me and hurting me.

I sifted the flour into the bowl and added a pinch of salt. I crossed the kitchen and opened the fridge and stared in, wondering what Catherine had been doing these last few years and what it was I needed in the fridge.

No doubt she'd been steadily climbing her ladder of success, leaving lesser mortals by the wayside. She was what you might call an exceptional woman, a high achiever. She had been groomed for the top, and the top was where she was heading.

Margarine. I drifted back to my bowl and dropped a cold chunk of it into the flour and clouds drifted up, dusting my sleeves with their ghostly particles. Catherine's parents had encouraged her, nurturing each interest or small talent as it showed itself. There had been piano lessons and day trips to the Tate and the National Gallery. Many a happy hour had been spent with Daddy in the Science Museum and many a happy week in Greece and France and once, the USA. She had ballet lessons for the grace and discipline it would bestow on her in later life. And her very own pony so that she could learn to conquer and control.

I rubbed the fat into the flour and the salt into my wounds. I wished her ladder hadn't crossed my path. Did she mistake me for a snake, I wondered? A slippery snake that might drag her back to square one?

How did it happen? How did I fall from grace and glory? Was I a cat who thought she could not only look at kings and queens, but live among them and be their equal? My rage grew as I mixed water into the mixture, stirring it and moulding it. The child in me was wailing, 'It isn't fair!' and I kneaded the pastry and pounded it like dough and ruined it. I sighed and dropped it in the bin and began yet again. It must be the best for Catherine, only the very best would do.

At first we'd had very little contact. Put simply, she dealt in words and I in pictures. It wasn't that I couldn't deal with words, it was more that in my view each painting or photograph existed in its own right without the need for the props of words. Perhaps I relied too heavily on intuition, yet more often than not it paid off.

My intuition let me down as far as Catherine was concerned; I'd trusted her completely. I'd told her things about myself that I could barely tell my best friend. She was like that; she had this power, she could draw out even the darkest secrets. And yet all the time she withheld her own truths.

One evening I was working late, hanging the pictures for an exhibition that was due to open the following afternoon. I had propped each painting against the wall and I was sitting in the middle of the room considering how well the arrangement worked. Catherine came in quietly, smiling and nodding approval as she looked around.

'You must be tired.'

I shook my head. 'Not really.'

'It looks wonderful. You do have an eye for this. I'm sure I couldn't do it.'

'It's the paintings that are wonderful. It doesn't take much skill to hang them.'

'Are you planning on staying much longer? I really fancy a drink and I'm almost done in the office.'

We went to a pub near the tube station and found a table away from the darts players and the juke-box and chatted about the gallery. Then, somehow, I found myself telling her all these very private and difficult things about my life. She made a big deal of everything. Telling me what a hard time I'd had of it and what a strong woman I must be. I told her about my mother dying and how my father drank, and about the evil step-mum.

I was careful this time with the pastry. I got sick of Wagner and put on some Johnny Cash instead. The songs he sang were so mournful they always had the effect of making me feel quite happy. I sprinkled flour on the Formica surface of the table and began to roll out the mixture. There is something very satisfying, creative even, about rolling out pastry; taking a misshapen lump and turning it into something flat and thin and delicate.

I wondered what kind of cook Catherine was. I knew she gave smart dinner parties, but that didn't mean that she was a good cook. I suddenly realised that I was still looking for something I could outdo her at.

Pathetic.

I greased the dish and draped the limp sheet of pastry over the bottom. I spooned the fruit in and sprinkled it with sugar than peered closely at the berries. Something seemed to move. I poked around but could distinguish no wriggling maggoty thing hiding there. What did it matter anyway?

I suddenly felt ashamed of myself. What did I think I was doing? She was still making a fool of me. Still making me prove to the world what a rotten crawling parasite I was.

I picked up one of the blackberries and brushed away the sugar. I could see nothing wrong with it. I popped it in my mouth, almost fearing its poison; my poison. It was a little overripe – its taste was blandly innocent. I ate another. This time it was not ripe enough and was hard and sharp. I ate another and another and another, until they were all gone. I thought about going into the garden to fetch some more, but I couldn't be bothered. In the cupboard I found a tin of cherry-pie filling that I'd been saving for a rainy day – I opened it. It was thick and gelatinous and over-sweet, and dropped from the spoon in great cloying globules. I covered it quickly with the rest of the pastry and popped it in the oven.

I thought about how it had all started. How we'd had those chats in the pub more and more often. She was so interested in what I had to say and so keen to know. 'She took photographs? I thought she was just a model, a beautiful hanger on!'

So I'd tell her all I knew.

I gave her a potted history of women artists of the world in twenty easy lessons. I lent her my favourite books and told her which exhibitions were worth seeing. I thought I was her teacher. Then, one day at a meeting, I'd been talking about a show we were hoping to put on later that year when she interrupted me.

'Excuse me. I'm sorry, but did you just say that Tina Modatti was the lover of Alfred Stieglitz? Don't you mean Edward Weston?' Everyone turned to look at her. She was smiling benignly. I stood silently wondering how she could know more than me. She continued, 'Or perhaps you were referring to Georgia O'Keeff, who was the lover of Stieglitz?'

By then I had lost my thread entirely and couldn't remember who I was talking about or why. 'Or Dorothy Norman, also a lover of Stieglitz?' She paused, then added in a throw-away, sardonic tone, 'Quite a guy, old Stieglitz.' A ripple of laughter went round the room. I blushed and stuttered and tried to continue the talk, but the momentum was gone. Jenny, bless her heart, suggested we all have coffee. I never did finish that talk and the idea was forgotten.

The smell of baking filled the kitchen as I cleared away the bowls and wooden spoons and weighing scales. It was getting late and I began to feel tiredness washing over me in great waves. I heard the front door slam and loud voices in the hall. I felt caught in the act; guilty of, I don't know what.

When I next saw Catherine she said nothing about the incident at the meeting. Instead she asked me if there were any good books on a photographer she'd just heard of called Diane Arbus. I said no. Why should I feed her information if all she was going to do was use it against me? At home I had three excellent books on Arbus, and a quantity of magazine and journal articles, and home, I decided, was just where they were going to stay.

Paul and Richard came into the kitchen to make coffee. They were swaying about and laughing. 'What's that lovely smell, Susan?'

'Ooo, smells great, Susan. Give us a bit.'

'No, it's for a friend.'

'Oh, we're not your friends then, eh?'

'You're drunk.' I said taking it out of the oven, all golden and steaming.

'And you're a great cook.'

Flattery always gets me. The pie was delicious.

Hatred can burn inside you. It can stick to the roof of your mouth like hot jam. It will hurt for days. Best thing to do is spit it out as fast as you can.

I felt a bit mean about the Arbus books. After all I had made the mistake about Tina Modatti's lover. Catherine had been right to correct me. I started to think I should say something like, 'Who were you asking about yesterday? Did you say Abbott or Arbus?' Then she would repeat her question and I could offer her the books and salve my conscience.

I realised that Jenny was right – the past was the past. What happened couldn't be changed or re-written. Poison pies and devil spit and spitefulness didn't help me then, but brought about my downfall, maybe it would do the same now.

If only I hadn't lied about the books. I just couldn't believe it when I heard about the new exhibition and who was going to organise it.

'Susan. Guess what?'

Jenny had come rushing into the gallery, nearly falling over herself in her excitement.

'What?'

'You know the New York Museum that put on the "Two Centuries Two Hundred Women" show?'

'Yes.'

'They're lending us the Arbus collection. It's brilliant, isn't it? Catherine got it. I can't believe it. It'll be one of the best things we've ever done!'

'Arbus?'

'Yes, Arbus. You know. Oh no, Catherine said you'd never heard of her. Well, she's really important. I'm surprised you'd never heard of her. Anyway, must run, I've got to tell the others.'

She turned to leave. I wanted to say that I did know. That I knew everything there was to know. That I'd loved that woman's work for ages. But no words came.

'Oh, by the way, you don't have to worry about all the

background stuff and research. Catherine knows it all, so she'll be curating. See you.'

I went to bed with a plan to cancel the meeting with Catherine. I decided it would hurt too much to see her, to hear all the wonderful things she'd been doing, to smile and smile and swallow my pride and anger.

What I dreamed that night I do not know, but I woke feeling happy with the world and cleansed of the past. I would meet Catherine and I'd smile real smiles. She couldn't hurt me any more. I was sure of that.

I decided my friendly gesture would be to buy her lunch. That would be enough; an unplanned, uncalculated offer of friendship.

We met at a wine bar of her choice. I sat at a table near the back and after ordering a glass of the house wine I settled down with a book. She was late as usual, but after twenty minutes I glanced up to see her moving briskly towards me, smiling and nearly sweeping everything from each table that she passed.

'You look wonderful.'

She bent and put her cheek next to mine and kissed the air at my ear. Then she sat down and waved an arm at the waiter who was suddenly and miraculously moved to an attentiveness he had not previously possessed. While he fetched the champagne which she insisted she was going to treat us to, she rummaged through her bag and produced a large gift-wrapped package. The bow wafted elegantly as she passed the be-ribboned box over the table to me.

'Oh Susan, I hope you don't mind, I just had to get you a little gift. For old times. I want you to know how much I think of you. You're very special, you know.'

I took the parcel from her, too shocked to protest. Too embarrassed by the unequal exchange to even thank her. Irony and contradiction danced in my wine-fuddled head.

'Well open it,' she urged, 'only be careful.'

She watched me intently as I untied the satin bow and peeled back the expensive paper to reveal a box.

'Oops. Keep it upright!'

The thing inside the box felt heavy and cold. I struggled to open it. Catherine watched over me like a beneficent mother hen. She clucked as I struggled to free my gift, and cooed when it was finally released.

I placed it on the table before me. It was a beautiful, and clearly expensive, glass dessert dish, and inside it was an artful swirl of pale lilac and syrupy purple.

'It's a crème anglais with a blackberry and Kirsch coulis,' she said sweetly, 'I made it myself. I even picked the berries . . . specially . . . Just for you . . .'

NIGHT OF THE TWISTERS

~

Elizabeth Ashworth

The film would pass an hour. Anna had a virus, so could use that as an excuse to watch, on this warm summer evening. Although the critic in her expected sentimental garbage – the story was about a wholesome American family, almost destroyed by a tornado hit – she acknowledged that this was her main reason for switching on – the family part, anyway.

The first frames of the film contained a tableau of clean-cut youngsters in early romance, at swings in a park. A light breeze was blowing. But as the boy unburdened to a girl the details of a quarrel with his father, leaves suddenly began scuttering and trees to sough. Weather forecasters grew perturbed: gales strengthened, ominous clouds scudded.

The phone rang, but Anna didn't pick it up, choosing to listen instead to the message as it played.

She was hearing the voice of the husband she had abandoned.

Ostensibly, he was thanking her for the tape – readings of some poems and prose – which she had recorded for him. Anna and he had once enjoyed the amused, ironic tone of this writer: his iconoclasm. They had discovered him together, when they were art students.

She soon understood that the phone call was subtly to warn her that he would be in her home town from tonight, at his old studio, with his girlfriend, another painter. 'Her place is immaculate,' he said, while fondly complaining to Anna once about the girl's painterly obsessiveness. 'She's forever scrubbing and bleaching the floorboards – down on her hands and knees for hours, before she starts any work.'

This made Anna remember the way he had kept his own materials and tools – his fastidious washing-out of the brushes with thick, sudsy soap, after their turpentine first cleansing. He'd shown her, with broad, competent hands, how to gently re-model the tan-coloured hairs into filbert shapes, and grade them in the jar, already full of fan-shapes, and the huge candles of bristle brushes. Languorously, he scoured the palette of surplus gobbets of paint, before burnishing it finally with a turpsy rag. Later, when they married, the smell of oil and spirit was always in their home.

Anna recalled, once more, her reason for leaving him, still wondering if she had been a coward, still confused by his arguments, still unsure of the rightness of her decision. She graphically reminded herself of a past whose pains had dimmed, like those of childbirth, leaving only apprehension, and a faint dread.

Yet, when he talked of Esther, her heavy mane of hair, her vanity, her possessiveness and jealousy, Anna yearned to be that girl.

With his voice as accompaniment, she returned to the tornado beginning to form on the screen, in what was being described as a 'screwdriving' cloud, which had earthed itself, before annihilating every obstacle to its passage. The film family was in crisis, blown apart by circumstance, kept apart by the meteorological phenomenon: emotion rising in their breasts, helping them realise the importance of one another, and eclipsing those trivial differences which had threatened their closeness. The producers weren't kidding when they'd called the film *Night of the Twisters*. There were eleven tornado hits in all, with a montage of newsreels providing the necessary authentic feel. She watched cars fly, roofs tear apart, windows implode. After many tests of courage, revealing the moral worth of each family member, they were reunited: homeless, but wiser and fundamentally reconciled.

She switched the television off, put the mewing cat out, and ran an early bedtime bath. Through the clear deeps of the water, when she pulled the plug out, Anna could feel its urgent force and see the almost solid spiral she had created, as it drained away.

Pushing in her big toe, to break through the vortex, she sensed that queer, blind, sucking power, and drew away quickly, in gleeful dismay. It filled her with the same excitement and terror as it had when, to get her out of the bath, her parents had said she had the devil at her heels.

As she got into her nightie, she watched the silver, spinning top of water sway and disappear like a condemning, impervious genie.

'He saw us! He told her to run on ahead – she didn't even look at us! Then he forced a smile, and muttered something about having to fetch some luggage. He didn't speak again, after that.'

Her sister had stopped off with the news.

'What's she like?'

'Oh – typical girly art student, you know . . .'

'But he's gone fifty!'

'Looking good, though.'

She could imagine the scene: she knew where the grass had worn away, to make a bald shortcut to the trains; she'd often walked with him herself that way, when they were trying to sell his landscape paintings to the shops and hotels. The brushwork of those pictures was still fresh in her mind: the treatment of stone and sky, and the colours, lead greys and cold blues. She had been nineteen then, younger than this girl now.

Still dressed for bed, she waved her sister off, and, feverish and exhausted, closed the door.

Those few married years, whose events were branded vibrantly on her imagination, now seemed to catapult to oblivion, before her sight, in a flurry of indefinable colours and shapes.

The cat began its yowling, insistent as ever, outside. But the cry had a different quality tonight – it was more plangent, more broad and full, with an oddly salacious note that unnerved her and sent a sudden wave of misery over her heart. When she opened the door to let him in, he sat there, impassively, his eyes slightly glazed, as if he were drunk.

'Come on, puss. Come in, then.'

She was worried now – maybe he was sick? Usually he flew past her legs, without stopping, to see what food was out for him. She bent towards him, to gather him up and examine him, but he ducked her reach and tossed and threw something from his mouth, before slinking swiftly to a corner of the room to crouch tensely and trap, alternately, with tooth and paw, a writhing mouse. The creature was the same colour as the cat, almost a part of him, yet humbled and invalidated. The cat sparred, delicately and consummately, with all his expertise and style, as if taking the mouse deadly seriously. But he was merely toying with it, while gazing round in ennui. Anna watched, shocked, in her nightdress, cursing her idiocy in not understanding that unearthly cry.

'Out! Out!' she shooed, before scooping up the dying victim in a dustpan, and chucking it randomly over the flower beds.

The whole preposterous scene remained in her mind: the open door; the dead television; the carpeted interior; the cat's instinct to kill; the mouse's to free itself and find a hiding-place; the scent of the evening; the swift body soaring sightless over the blue catmint blossoms, lying like paper stars in a green night, and the rush of air in her ears, like a whirl-wind.

THE GREEN TREES BY THE RIVER

~

Ann Morus

The American Baptist choir spent the early hours of the morning running up and down the narrow passageway on the deck outside the cabin windows, whooping and shrieking at each other. When Elin finally got out of her bunk and tried to force shut her window, a ghostly face with perfect grinning teeth laughed at her as it floated past, and waved its white hands. The cabin window refused to move.

By daylight everything was calm again – the curling blue-grey water of the wide river, the rows of pale green poplars on either bank, the delicately swaying furls of the blue and yellow Ukrainian flag on the stern – and she wondered if she had dreamed it. On the passageway outside her window, two white plastic chairs were lying on their sides, with scrunched-up empty soft-drink cans rolling gently between them to the movement of the boat. When she returned from breakfast, chairs and cans had all been removed.

The group from Smith Liversage Tours were strolling down the wide dirt track from the landing stage to the museum on the hill. It was the first time they had been on land since they had left Kiev and Elin would have liked time to stand and look around her, but they were already behind schedule and Yelena the courier, walking at the back of the group to discourage stragglers, kept looking surreptitiously at her watch.

'Do we have to climb all the way up *there* to the museum?' Peter, walking near the back of the group, asked of the world in general.

'Of course. It is the Shevchenko Museum. Today was his birthday,' said Yelena. Her voice was patient. 'You remember, I spoke about him last evening?'

'The one who hid bits of paper in his boots?'

'Well, yes. He wrote poetry in the Ukrainian language at a time when to the educated people it was just a peasant language – he criticised the political system – the Tsar sent him to exile in Kazakstan and forbade him to write poetry – so he wrote his poems on small pieces of paper and put them in his big boots.'

Silence, exile and cunning again, thought Elin; and the greatest of these is cunning. 'Brave man,' she said.

Yelena looked gratified. Peter looked bored. Chesney Leith, striding out at the front of the group, turned back to stare, her thin smile sharp at the edges, and said, 'Now, Elin, you're *identifying* again. Elin, you see,' she explained slowly and carefully to Yelena, 'comes from a place called *Wales*, which is on one side of England, and she speaks *Welsh*. Now some people from *Wales* think that they and their language have been badly treated by the cruel and oppressive *English*, who imprison them without trial and torture them and send them into exile without time off for good behaviour – just like the Tsar, really. So they fight back bravely by going around with paintbrushes and tins of green paint as a sign of defiance, and if they wore big boots I'm sure they'd stuff little pieces of paper down them just like Shevchenko.'

'This is a joke?' asked Yelena, looking interested. 'Or is it true?' The rest of the group were all grinning broadly, their eyes bright like spectators at a fist-fight, watching Elin to see how she reacted.

'Yes,' she said with a straight face. 'And Welsh pigs can fly—'

There was general polite amusement. Everyone relaxed. They ambled on.

I should, thought Elin, be better prepared. Now that it's unfashionable to get at the Irish it seems to be our turn for attention. And I went along with her terms. I acquiesced. If this is the way it's going to be for the whole trip, I need to think of some way to get back at her. I need cunning. Exile doesn't really come into it here and silence I can do, but I need to work on the cunning . . .

It had started on the journey out. The Smith Liversage group (still, at this stage, a collection of individuals who didn't know each other) were in the transit lounge in Zurich, waiting for the flight to Kiev; Elin was re-reading *Traed Mewn Cyffion*, one of the set-books she'd be teaching the following year. Another member of the group, a woman with glossy pale-brown hair and a body like a tall old-fashioned cupboard with ill-fitting doors, who had been striding up and down between the rows of seats, suddenly stopped in front of Elin, sat down next to her, looked with open curiosity at the book she was reading, and immediately asked, 'Oh, can you read Ukrainian?' The moment the words left her mouth she said, 'Ah, no – wrong alphabet,' and when Elin said, 'It's Welsh,' she had immediately exclaimed that her parents had had a holiday home near Aberdaron for years, 'until the security situation deteriorated,' and that now she looked at it closely *of course* she could see it was Welsh. The mistake, however, had been made – and to a stranger, who would not be forgiven.

The air was soft and bright. Elin felt warm and alive in her skin. In the long pale grass between the path and the trees, a blonde girl in a gold bikini was doing gymnastic contortions on a small table; under the trees, a man in Ukrainian national costume played the accordion – it sounded like a folk-song made for dancing – while another, with a floppy black moustache, juggled dumb-bells while walking on a tight-rope strung between two of the trees. The man with the accordion began to sing; his warm baritone floated across the golden summer stillness to the Smith Liversage party as they straggled on, crunching small stones underfoot.

'Better watch out,' said Chesney. 'They'll be asking for money on the way back.'

'Given the choice,' said Julian Leith, 'who would you rather be? What would you rather be doing, given the choice?' They were in the ship's bar and he was leaning on the bar-counter; the angle of his body strengthened the impression Elin had had when she first saw him, of a candle whose shape, once tall and straight, had been thickened over the years by the fat globules of running wax as the candle burned and his life melted away. He had the expression of an ageing pale-haired cherub who could still not understand why the world around him had not after all been arranged for his benefit, and this seemed to include his wife. ('Chesney and Julian,' Peter had said shortly after they sailed from Kiev, 'are like that little wooden man and woman who go in and out of a little wooden house to predict the weather. When she's around in the day, he's sleeping it off in his cabin; when he's in the bar in the evening, she's having an early night. You never see them together.')

'The choir's away giving a concert somewhere tonight,' said Martin, anxious to avoid hypotheticals. 'They won't be back till tomorrow.'

'Praise the Lord,' said Julian, grinning. He finished his vodka. 'And pass some more ammunition, Dmitri, for me and my friends. When you're ready.' The barman, smiling at no one in particular, refilled their glasses.

'You haven't,' said Julian looking at Elin, 'told me about all the exciting places you saw today. Some poet or something?'

'Shevchenko,' said Elin.

'Bless you,' said Julian automatically. 'Give that woman a Kleenex.' He chuckled.

'Never mind,' said Martin. 'Tomorrow we're going to see a collective farm.'

Elin was falling deep, into nothing; the white terrified faces of people she knew floated around her in the darkness. Paul's face, hurt and frightened, came past her. His mouth moved as if he was saying something and his eyes were dark and staring, fixed on her as he went past: don't leave me don't leave me . . . I am falling, I am falling. This is the bottomless pit.

And then she woke up, and realised that the boat was truly falling and it must be the deep lock, the deepest in Europe, and she had missed being on deck with all the others to watch the dark concrete walls of the lock get higher and higher as the boat sank on the falling water and at breakfast it would be 'Oh, but you should have seen it. Pity you missed it.' I didn't miss it, she thought. I felt it in my bones.

The visit to the collective farm overran because the school-children's display of folk-dancing lasted too long ('Truly epic,' said Chesney when Yelena asked her if she had enjoyed it) and when they finally went to rejoin their coach it had disappeared along with all the jackets and carrier bags they'd left in it. Yelena vanished in a taxi and they sat on the school steps in the sun watched at a distance by politely curious villagers. ('I'm not surprised,' said Chesney. 'They must think we've come from Mars. Anyone got any wampum?')

Yelena returned with their lost property. The coach had broken down and temporary repairs had failed; they would have to wait for a replacement. Martin produced a packet of peppermints and handed them round the group. He then offered them to the nearest villagers, who grinned and shook their heads. 'They're *English* sweets,' he said, hurt.

The replacement coach arrived, old, battered and making kangaroo-leaps in the potholes. They all clambered on. Now that the strangers were safely corralled, the villagers came closer, smiling and waving as the coach jolted off. We came to look at them like animals in a zoo, thought Elin, and they're doing it back to us. They know who *they* are in this place: *we're* the ones who are freaks. The bus swerved wildly to avoid a chicken and nearly skidded off the road. 'Only another ten miles to go,' said Chesney, and laughed.

When they were back on board having lunch, it was first announced that the afternoon visit to the 'typical village' would go ahead, but later than originally planned; then that it had been cancelled; finally that the boat would stop there for half an hour, to allow a quick glimpse to those who wanted it.

Elin, looking from the mercilessly hot deck at the deep green shade of the trees near the landing stage on the left bank, decided to go. No one else seemed very interested. The track led up to a high earth bank and then curved to the right between tall, pale green, waving fronds. At the entrance to the village there was a line of poplars. The earth was rich and dark, brickhard on the garden paths, crumbling in the vegetable beds. Nearly every garden had trees; small fruits – some pale yellow, others a deep purplish-blue – glistened between the leaves. The houses were made of old weathered wood; inside the open doors, the rooms looked cool and dark. A dog lying across a threshold raised its head as she passed, then sank back on to its paws again.

'Mad dogs and Englishwomen,' said a familiar clipped voice behind her: Chesney Leith, sensible pale-brown bob swinging as she strode along, hands in the pockets of her dull-pink denim skirt, camera slung over the shoulder of her sensible pink-and-lilac Liberty-print shirt. At the sound of her voice, the dog sat up on its haunches and looked at her warily.

'It wasn't suspicious of *you*.' She sounded amused. 'It's as if it thinks you're one of the natives. Do you feel an affinity?' And she stared at Elin, her eyes full of malice and insolence. Elin smiled back angrily. 'Not with the dog,' she said, and turned on her heel and started walking back the way she had come. Behind her Chesney's clear voice cut mockingly through the soft air. 'Well, *I'm* going to look at the rest of it even if *you're* not game. I'm sure there's heaps more to see!'

Elin walked fast and resentfully back along the track. The moment – the perfect warmth and golden silence of the afternoon in the village – had been broken. She was angry with Chesney for breaking it, angry with herself for letting it be broken. The pale green waving fronds no longer looked magical.

The ship's hooter sounded faintly. She walked faster, and had nearly reached the high earth bank when she realised that if the hooter had sounded faint to her, it must have been completely inaudible to Chesney somewhere on the other side of the village. *Good,* she thought. As she approached the landing stage she saw that the crew were preparing to cast off, and the officer by the gangway was making frantic arm-movements to her to hurry up. All the other passengers seemed to be either on the boat or the gangway. I suppose I should tell them about Chesney. Suppose I should make them wait.

'You almost miss the boat,' said the officer, smiling. He took her arm to help her on to the gangway, and followed her on to the boat. The gangway swung back on to the deck, the ropes were released. The boat started to move away from the landing-stage.

She went down to her cabin. Too late now for second thoughts: speaking too late was worse than saying nothing. On her bunk lay the cruise map; just beyond this point, she saw, the river made a wide bend, almost two-thirds of a circle, before reaching the next stopping-point in mid-evening. Someone travelling by road would be able to cut off the bend and reach the next stopping-point before the boat arrived.

No problem. Chesney can show us how resourceful the ex-Head Girl of an English private school can be.

She sat back on the bunk, reassured. An unpleasant few hours for Chesney, maybe, but no great harm done. It could even be described as character-building, if Chesney's character had not been so immovably cemented into place already. She went up on deck. There was a faint breeze as the boat moved through the water; only the leaves on the fringes of the tall trees on the banks quivered gently.

The boat juddered and slowed. She crossed to the other side of the deck. The boat was moving towards a small stone landing-stage on the left bank of the river.

It must be Chesney. Drawing on the finely-honed skills of a Cub Scout leader, she must have found a phone, somehow contacted the boat, commandeered a tractor, a droshky, a donkey, *something*, and terrified the owner into taking her to this hidden unofficial stopping-place. Elin felt huge relief – and underneath it, profound disappointment. The spirit that built an empire had won through. She's defeated the natives again.

And then she saw that all the figures approaching the landing-stage from the shelter of the nearby trees were dressed in jeans and white tee-shirts with a slogan in Ukrainian and an American flag on the front and the logo of a dove and flames on the back. Some of them carried instrument cases, and many of the men walked in pairs carrying sections of staging between them. More and more of them emerged from under the trees, chatting to each other, glancing casually towards the boat – which clung, engine throbbing and eager to leave, to the landing-stage – and continued to saunter towards the gangway where the officer was anxiously trying to hurry them on board.

It took a long time. All the staging had to be carefully carried aboard and stowed on the bow deck, and even when this was completed there were still choir members emerging nonchalantly from the trees and ambling towards the gang-way and the increasingly desperate officer. There was no sign of Chesney. Finally the gangway was raised and the boat eased itself quickly back into the centre of the river.

So it would be the next scheduled stop after all, round the bend of the river, in the small town whose cultural centre was presenting an entertainment for them after dinner. Would Chesney be waiting when they landed or appear during the performance?

Elin started to get ready for dinner. The full-dress number tonight, she thought: the perfume, the jade silk, the turquoise and silver. I have something to celebrate.

No one at dinner seemed to notice Chesney's absence; it was as if everyone assumed she was at another table and wasn't interested enough to check. Julian had apparently been in the bar since late afternoon, continually saying he'd better get something to eat but then deciding to have another drink first. Everyone wondered gloomily whether the visit to the cultural centre would feature yet more folk-dancing.

Then Yelena appeared with an announcement. The boat had lost so much time during the day, first with their delay in returning from the farm and then by picking up the choir, that it was in danger of losing its place in the queue for the next lock. Therefore, with regret, the visit to the cultural centre had been cancelled. She apologised very much for their disappointment. The boat would sail straight on.

Elin sat back, looking at her empty coffee-cup. Peter and the others were all going off to the bar 'to celebrate temporary freedom from folk-dancing'. She joined them. She had a drink. She started to enjoy herself. When someone asked her what the 'typical village' had been like, she said merely that it had been old and very quiet. None of them mentioned Chesney. Certainly Julian, his face like a mis-shapen pink pudding, had been well beyond noticing anyone's presence or absence for some time. After he had slumped forward over the bar for the third time, the barman approached their table and said anxiously to Peter, who was leaning across the table to talk to Elin, 'I think maybe it is better if you take your friend to bed.'

'Ah,' said Peter as if caught out, and then, 'Ah, *Julian.* Right.' He looked across to the bar. 'Yes, I see what you mean. What about his cabin keys, though? Anyone know if Chesney locks the door?' Martin spluttered into his glass.

'He has his keys,' said the barman. 'He has put them by his drink.'

Peter and Martin, it was finally agreed, would carry Julian down to his cabin. Which, of course, could be a problem: Chesney, it was well known, went to bed very early and could be expected to be already asleep. Elin offered to join them; she could, she suggested, go into the cabin first and reassure Chesney (if she was still awake) that the men about to stagger into her cabin carrying a large heavy object between them were no cause for alarm. 'Good thinking, Batman,' said Peter.

Julian started to slide gracefully down to the floor.

As she stood up, lifting the strap of her shoulder-bag from the back of her chair, a sudden visual memory flashed in front of her. Chesney in the village, grinning insolently at her, dressed in her sensible print shirt and her sensible denim skirt, with her camera slung over her shoulder *and nothing else.* No bag. Nowhere she could have kept money, passport or map. Nowhere she could have carried anything to show the people in the silent village where she wanted to go, or the dollars to pay them to take her there, or anything to prevent her being stranded in a strange and alien place without any immediate means of getting out of it.

Manoeuvring Julian's inert figure down the narrow spiral staircase took nearly fifteen minutes and provided on-board cabaret for the nearby passengers, who applauded enthusiastically when he was finally manhandled down to the right corridor (Julian himself remained completely unconscious throughout). Elin walked ahead of them with Julian's keys and let herself into the cabin, shutting the door quietly behind her.

The bright lights of the corridor, the noise of the passengers, the muttered complaints and instructions of Peter and Martin were all left behind. The cabin was dark and silent; there was only a weak light from the window and the faint soft sounds of the river as the boat moved through the water. On the right-hand bunk was a man's shirt, red and crumpled; the left one held a brown leather shoulderbag and a pink cardigan. Elin quickly and quietly drew the curtains around the left bunk so that it was completely hidden. As she turned back towards the door, something outside the cabin window caught her eye as it went past: a pale face against the darkness, looking curiously into the cabin and laughing as it went past. Must have been one of the choir.

She turned back and went into the corridor, leaving the cabin door ajar. She put her finger to her lips and pointed to the curtained bunk. Peter and Martin nodded and then quietly carried Julian into the cabin and without touching the curtains lowered him carefully onto the right-hand bunk. They took off his shoes, put them on the floor under the bunk, and then loosened his belt. Peter put the cabin keys on the small ledge under the window and they all withdrew to the corridor, closed the door, and leaned against the corridor walls, grinning at each other with relief at a job well done.

'Mission accomplished,' said Martin, 'and we all deserve a drink.' They went back up the stairs to the bar to join the others.

Martin got the drinks. Peter began a long and detailed account of how, at great personal effort and inconvenience, they had got Julian down the staircase and crammed into his bunk. And Elin finally relaxed, and laughed with the others; she leant back luxuriously into the deep velvet chair, raised her ice-cold glass of vodka, and drank a silent toast to Taras Shevchenko.

THE SEVENTH WAVE

~

Pamela Cockerill

Lucy glared at the waves breaking meekly at her feet, not daring to wash over her sensible sandals and white ankle socks. 'Seventh wave, seventh wave, make our hotel disappear,' she muttered, counting carefully. But the wave, when it came, was as feeble as the preceding ones, and though she repeated the wish as it broke, it was without hope.

She scowled into the sun. Everything was dull here compared to Rhossili. What was her best friend doing now? Searching rock pools for jelly fish? Creeping down the slippery grass track to Blue Pool? Surfing beachwards on the foaming Gower waves?

Elinor. El-in-oah. She rolled the name around in her head recapturing the voices of the Lloyd family who owned the caravan next to theirs. 'El-in-oah!' 'Yes marmeah?' Their words soared and dipped like seabirds. Her own mother laughed when she tried to copy them. 'You've got to live in Welsh Wales to have a lovely accent like that.'

Mr and Mrs Lloyd sang in the chapel choir on Sundays. Sometimes Lucy woke in the morning to the sound of their harmonizing. 'Amazing grace how sweet the sound that saved a wretch like me . . .' Elinor had translated the Welsh for her. The caravan seemed too small to hold all that singing and the voices flowed through every window, soaring away with the seagulls.

'Lucinda! Don't get your feet wet, it's almost time for

lunch.' Her grandmother's voice cut through the pictures in her head. Walking along the promenade that trapped the tidy beach of the Devon resort, she hoped Grandma wouldn't meet anyone she knew. A vain hope, since she, and it seemed, everyone else in their hotel, had been coming to the same resort for forty years.

Sure enough a large lady with a red face waved and would have stopped, but Grandma said, 'Good day, Ursula,' and hurried past. Lucy scuffed her toes in the sand trapped in gutters.

Grandma bit days into neat pieces just like she ate sandwiches. First a long bath, then breakfast, then a walk along the prom, then one hour on the beach because of Lucy. Lucy sensed she hadn't wanted to bring her any more than she had wanted to come, but Grandma was hot on doing her duty.

It was all Smudge's fault.

At Rhossili time didn't matter. They stayed on the beach until the sun went down or the tide turned or until they were too hungry to stay any longer. Rhossili was her favourite place in all the world and Elinor was her favourite friend. The sea hissed and sucked beyond the sand dunes and on wet days she could watch the clouds of drizzle blot out Worm's Head on the left of the beach and Burry Holm on the right.

Once her mother had told her that on a stormy night, Worm's Head had chopped itself off the mainland and sailed out to sea to look for its lost body. That night Lucy dreamt she was alone on an island drifting far from land. She woke up crying, and her mother had squashed into her bunk to cuddle her back to sleep. There wouldn't be room for that now that Smudge was growing inside her stomach.

Grandma met a lady she *did* like and stopped to talk. Lucy studied the buckets and spades in a shop window and listened. '. . . a bit tedious but what can one do? Her mother needs complete bed rest and can't be expected to cope with a six year old and my son is away on business. Yes, it's their first baby . . .'

There it was again. First baby. When Grandma had been told about the expected baby she'd said, 'But you're much too old for a first baby!' Her mother had put her arms right around Lucy and said, 'This is my first baby.' And Grandma had said crossly, 'You know what I mean and Lucinda knows that she's adopted.'

Of course she knew. She'd always known the story of how her mother and father had waited and waited for a baby and then specially chosen her. But now there was a brother, Smudge, snug and close in her mother's stomach at home in Cardiff and now her mother wasn't well enough to climb sand dunes and surf in the rolling green Gower waves that patterned the sands with great necklaces of seaweed.

'Whatever were you thinking of?' Grandma had said, and her mother had laughed and said, 'Not a lot at the time!' Then Grandma got two pink spots on her cheeks and her lips went thin and mauve where the lipstick stopped. 'Thirty-nine. It's not safe.'

'I'm a perfectly healthy woman. You were almost my age when you had Ian.'

'The risks are not just to the mother.'

'I'm having all the tests.'

One of the tests showed a picture of the baby. A magic machine called a scanner took a photograph that didn't look like anything to Lucy, but her father had pointed to a fuzzy shape and said, 'And that's the smudge that says it's a boy. You'll have a little brother.' Then he had laughed and smoothed her mother's hair and told her she was clever.

'You can choose his name,' her mother promised, but Lucy

couldn't think of a boy's name she liked. Boys in school were called David or Ben or Henry but she didn't think they would be right for Smudge. If it had been a girl she would have chosen Elinor and taught her to sing *Calon Lân* and told her about Worm's Head sailing out to sea and cuddled her if she had bad dreams . . . but a boy . . . 'Come along, Lucinda, we'll be late for lunch,' her grandmother said, as if *she* had been the one to stop and talk.

They smelt the burning before they turned the corner. Thick columns of black smoke were pouring from the windows. Grandma tightened her grip on Lucy's hand and gave a little scream. 'Our hotel! It's on fire!'

It had worked. Again. The first time had been at Rhossili when Mr Lloyd had promised fifty pence for the best sand castle. Elinor had built hers near the sea and found shells and feathers and a cardboard tube just the right shape for a tower. Lucy had looked from Elinor's castle to her own and out of nowhere the words had come. 'Seventh wave, seventh wave, make Elinor's castle disappear.' Then she had counted the waves and the seventh one had swelled up larger than the rest and crashed right over the beautiful castle. Lucy and Elinor had shared the fifty pence, but Lucy had lived with a bad feeling in her stomach for a long time.

Grandma let go her hand and ran forward with small tripping steps. 'My jewellery! My clothes!' A policeman stopped her. 'Sorry, madam, but it's well alight at the back.'

They were taken to another hotel with some of the other guests. Lucy liked the new hotel. It was shabby and friendly and they ate in a conservatory with huge grubby windows. Some of the guests from the burning hotel went home but the rest clung together like survivors from some disaster. The big red lady called Ursula sat with her and Grandma for meals. Ur-syew-lar. Why did some names sound so pretty and some so ugly?

Grandma wouldn't go home until she could collect her jewellery from the hotel safe. She bought them both some new things but Lucy had to wear the same dress and socks for three days running and Grandma gave up telling her to keep clean.

Grandma seemed to shrink in the new hotel. Nothing pleased her. Her tea was cold. Her boiled egg too hard. There was a draught from a cracked window in the room they had to share, right at the top, where the shabby grey carpet gave way to an even shabbier brown one. No one remembered her name and there was never a *Times* newspaper, only ones with rude pictures.

But worst of all, for Grandma, was the old man, sitting in the corner of the conservatory with a plate of dry bread crusts on his table. 'What a very peculiar person,' Grandma said, the first time she saw him.

'It's that rogue eye,' Ursula said, without lifting her eyes from her rude paper, 'makes him look a bit odd.'

The old man flapped from his table to the window. His trousers were baggy at the knees and flared wide at the ankles and strained across his big belly. On his big sticking-out feet he wore dirty grey trainers without laces or socks. His cardigan hung, hairy and shapeless, stained from previous meals. His head was shiny and bald, the skin marked with brown spots, yet black hair sprang from his nostrils and ears and tufts forced their way through the gaps of his buttoned shirt. From the pile of bread balanced on a plate he flung piece after piece out of the window at the wheeling gulls and every time a bird caught a piece he turned to face the room, breathing noisily, as if waiting for applause.

'Don't stare, Lucinda,' Grandma said, but Lucy couldn't drag her eyes from the man. His right eye held hers steadily but the other one rolled wildly in its socket, unable to settle for more than a second. Lucy knew that he didn't mind her staring. That he *wanted* people to look. Sometimes he held on to the bread, daring the birds to take it from his hand, but they never did.

Other people went on eating or looked away, embarrassed, but Grandma was furious. 'That awful old man. Why don't they ask him to leave?' she hissed at Ursula. Lucy could see that Ursula, tutting over her newspaper, had forgotten he was there, but Grandma, even sitting with her back to him, seemed to know everything he was doing – shivering when he opened the window and closing her eyes at his noisy breathing.

Lucy could hardly eat for watching the birds. Wild, swooping, twisting, falling, arching their curved wings into the wind. The birds knew exactly how to move, she thought, not like the old man who knocked into furniture and leaned dangerously out of the window.

She longed to go closer. The weather had changed and sweeping rain battered against the glass, but still he went on feeding the birds. He filled Lucy's days with a dangerous excitement with his mad rolling eye and his frantic attempts to tame the wicked gulls who shattered the air with their harsh 'Kwar! Kwar!' as they squabbled. Sometimes they seemed to be attacking him and Lucy could imagine the boldest one plucking out his mad eye and swallowing it, whole.

One morning Grandma could stand no more and called the waiter over. 'Could you possibly ask that gentleman to close the window?'

The waiter smirked and leaned closer. 'That's the old boss, madam.'

'I beg your pardon?'

'It's Himself. The present boss's father. He lives here.'

'Well! That explains a lot.' Her grandmother wiped her mouth with a paper serviette and said, 'Ursula, please keep an eye on Lucinda. I am going to phone my daughter-in-law.'

Ursula grunted and went on reading. The old man sent mad happy winks towards Lucinda. She smiled back, then, taking her hard boiled egg, tapped it against the side of her plate and picked all the shell off. Ursula didn't look up. Putting the egg into a bread roll, Lucy slipped from the table and went to where the old man was leaning out of the window.

She watched the birds outlined against the darker grey of the sky, riding the wind high over seventh and seventh and seventh waves. 'That's Lloyd,' he said suddenly, without looking round, as a more daring one circled ever nearer his outstretched hand. His voice was gravel, shifting. He turned and looked at her with his good eye. 'After Lloyd George. You'd be too young to know about him. A bugger for the women.'

Lucy silently played with the words, 'A bugger for the women.' Bugger was a bad word, she knew, but there was something else. Something that made the old man wheeze deep inside his chest. Laughter fighting to get out, like Mr and Mrs Lloyd's singing. Lloyd George. So Lloyd could be a first name as well. She handed him the wrapped egg and he took it in his thick fingers, peered inside and let the laughter escape. 'Don't blame you. Bloody awful things boiled eggs.'

As he leaned again into the wind, Lucy pleaded silently, 'Seventh wave, seventh wave, make the bird called Lloyd take the bread.' The big bird was so close that she could see the wind sifting the softer, darker feathers of his underwings, see the strongly quilled black feathers at the spreading wing tips. Then *she* was a bird, the wind flattening her feathers, lifting her as she rode the air, swearing harshly like them, as the old man laughed and taunted.

Then the bird came so close that Lucy looked into his unblinking yellow eye and held her breath as the cruel beak opened, but the old man's hand stayed steady as the gull dipped and snatched, taking the whole bread roll and egg together and swooping away. Lucy laughed and clapped and the old man, turning, caught and held her with his good eye and she knew that he too had been a bird. That he too could fly.

'Lucinda!' Her grandmother had angry red patches on her neck but she wasn't looking at Lucy. She was looking at the old man. For a long moment they stared at each other and the red patches darkened. Then the old man said loudly, 'Yes, a bugger for the women!' and turned his back on Grandma, back to the soaring gulls.

'Come Lucinda, we have to pack. We're going home.'

Happily, Lucy followed her grandmother up the stairs, singing quietly to herself. 'Seventh wave, seventh wave, make my brother Lloyd a *bugger* for the women.'

SEEING THINGS

~

Chloë Heuch

'Are you really going to leave me?'

I don't answer. For the moment I want to listen to the old house. Understand the noises the stones are making, the calls of the shells in the garden, the high song of the birds in the trees.

'Don't go,' he says sadly. 'Can't you stay here and keep me company?'

'They say my sight'll be gone completely in six months.'

My husband considers this. I can hear him next to me as I run my palm along the warm, irregular surface of the house wall and imagine its whiteness. We turn left, walk the seven steps into the garden to smell the fuchsia.

'If you went, where would you go?'

'Colwyn Bay, to be close to Ben and his wife. They've decided to call our grandson Dylan, after you.'

'Colwyn Bay? You'd hate it.'

'I'll have neighbours and a corner shop. Just think, there'll be buses that stop outside the front door. I'll be able to go to cafés and sit and drink tea.'

'But we bought this house for you.' He pauses. 'Don't you love me anymore?'

We renovated the house bit by bit. We made it beautiful. We made the garden what it is now, barrowing rich earth on to the acid soil until our hands blistered. I planted flowers: geraniums, clematis, pansies, even lilies, so a spectrum of colour would last us right through the spring and summer.

'Ben doesn't like me being up here. He says it's dangerous.'
'Mmm.'
'The last time I fell in the garden, I was there all night until the postman found me.'

Our home is half a mile from the nearest neighbour, but only five minutes from the sea: from the skyscraper cliff and the sound of the blue bay; the bliss of its wide stone mouth that blows cold kisses on my stone eyes. I haven't always been blind. I remember clearly the lapping tablecloth of aquamarine that is laid out to the edges of the horizon.

'So you will leave me then,' he says bitterly.
'Like you left me twenty years ago,' I retort.
'I came back as soon as I could.'
'It isn't the same. You ruined my life.'
'I never meant to.'
'After you had gone, everything began to lose focus.'

Relatives had come up the mountain to take away his clothes. Their itchy fingers pried at my grief; they thought they could load it all into bin-bags to hand over to Oxfam and Help the Aged. They thought that I could forget him. Move on. Move away.

'Every day, every day the pain is as fresh, as it was in the beginning.'
'I love you,' he whispers.
'When Sally Evans found your body on the beach, she came straight here. Her three greyhounds ran all over the flower beds. She knew it was you straight away, you had on the sheep-skin coat I'd made you. Three days of thinking you'd left me for that girl you worked with.'

My husband makes a noise like a cow's fart through his lips. He doesn't speak but walks a little away from me, down to the fence that overlooks the fields.

'You always run off when we have an argument,' I say quietly.

'You accused me of having an affair! With that – with that schoolgirl who stocked the shelves,' he snarls.

'But I thought I saw you together in the town. Then you were late home those times.'

'You were just seeing things that weren't there.'

I hear the creasing of his shirt as he crosses his arms and tucks his balled fists into his armpits, like he does when he is angry. I wish I could just touch him again, one more time put my arms around his waist.

'The ones from the village thought you'd tried to kill yourself.'

'It doesn't matter now.'

'I told them what the police said, it was an accident. Death by misadventure. It was in the paper. I've still got the cuttings.'

He walks back and sits beside me on the grass.

'Don't go,' he whispers to my guilt.

I don't reply. I can't speak. It's a long time before he rises again and paces back up the cobble-stone path, swishing this way and that, creating a small breeze. Over the teeth of the hawthorn is the beach. I can hear the soft rush-and-pause of the waves on the pebbles. It will be bone grey today, sunless dry pebbles and whittled sticks that look like carcass ribs the seagulls have cleaned and strewn over the mile long bay. I know what I have to do.

'I'm going now, Dyl.' I call into the air. Grief spills into my sentence and cracks the words. He is quiet, sulking in between the silver birches, watching me. I lock the house and count the steps to the front gate. I asked Ben not to wait too near the house so I could say goodbye properly. I can hear the engine turning over and the radio playing.

I reach the bend in the track and before the house is lost from view, I turn back to look out of habit, imagining the shape it makes on the side of the slate mountain. For a moment I can see again. I am not the only one who is leaving. The form of a giant grey bird slowly wings its way from the house, through the split between the mountain's giant thighs.

The moment passes and I am once again a blind old woman walking away, my sightless eyes brimming with the sea.

BIOGRAPHICAL NOTES

ELIZABETH ASHWORTH was born in Buxton, and now lives in Llanfairfechan in North Wales, where she teaches, writes and paints. She was awarded a Welsh Arts Council bursary in 1993 which enabled her to complete *So I Kissed Her Little Sister*, a novel published in 1999 by Parthian Books. Her poetry collection *A New Confusion* won the Alice Hunt Bartlett Prize, and her poems have appeared in *Poetry Wales*, *New Welsh Review*, *Outposts*, *Transatlantic Review* and *Poetry Review*. Her stories have been broadcast and published, and she has won second prize in the HE Bates short story competition. She is a Writer on Tour with The Welsh Academy, and works as a writer-in-residence with Conwy's Writing Squad, as well as in schools and community projects in Conwy.

LINDSAY ASHFORD was born in Wolverhampton in 1959. She worked as a radio journalist for the BBC and later went freelance, contributing to programmes like *Woman's Hour* and writing articles for national newspapers and women's magazines. She moved to Aberystwyth in 1997 and has just written her first novel. 'Charmed Life' is her first published story.

PAMELA COCKERILL lives in South Wales. She has had stories broadcast on Radio 4 and contributed regularly to magazines and anthologies. Five of her children's books have been published by Hodder & Stoughton, Canongate and Stabenfeldt and have appeared in Norway, Sweden, Denmark and Germany. She is a life-long member of SAMWAW (South & Mid Wales Association of Writers now approaching its 30th year). Twice runner-up in the Mathew Prichard Award, her latest book, *Finder's Keepers* is to be published by PONT in March 2000.

TESSA HADLEY was born in Bristol and has lived in Cardiff for 17 years. She was educated in Bristol and Cambridge and now works teaching English and Creative Studies at Bath Spa University College, consequently pays much too much towards the upkeep of the Second Severn Bridge. She has had several stories published in Honno anthologies before, and also broadcast on the radio; currently she is writing a book on Henry James.

CHRISTINE HARRISON was born on the Isle of Wight and lived in many different places before moving to Fishguard over twenty years ago. There she began writing short stories, winning several awards, notably the *Cosmopolitan* Short Story Award. In 1991 she was the recipient of a writer's bursary from the Welsh Arts Council. Her novel *Airy Cages* was published by Macmillan in 1994, and she is currently working on a collection of her short stories.

CHLOË HEUCH was born in Somerset in 1974. Her family, of Welsh/Yorkshire/Danish origin, moved to North Wales in 1987. She graduated from Lancaster University with an MA in Creative Writing, and is at present training to be a teacher. Her poems have been published in numerous magazines including, most recently, a batch of landscape poems in *Island*. 'Seeing Things' is her first published story.

ANNA HINDS is a poverty-stricken student at Cardiff University. Her story 'Holes in the Beach' was included in *Mama's Baby (Papa's Maybe)* (Parthian Books) and she has won *The Big Issue* 'poetas', and prizes for poetry and fiction in *The Western Mail* Young Writers Competition in 1998. Her greatest ambition in life is to receive a bank balance without an 'overdrawn' sign on it; and if she can't achieve that, she will be happy just to write forever.

CHRISTINE HIRST was born in Birmingham, but now lives in North Wales. Her family, originally from South Wales, lived in the Mountain Ash area. As a young woman she worked as a book reviewer and freelance journalist in Liverpool and later in Connah's Quay, North Wales. After moving to Shropshire, she became a teacher and headteacher, writing stories for children, before returning to North Wales to pursue her love of writing. She has been published in *Cambrensis* and was shortlisted for the Asham Award. She is currently working on a novel about Welsh convict women in Australia.

G. P. HUGHES was born and raised in Western Canada and worked in various Middle Eastern countries as a journalist and teacher before settling in Gwynedd 16 years ago. She has published in Canadian literary magazines and her stories have been broadcast on BBC Radio 4. Parthian Books are bringing out a collection of her stories in September 2000.

JO HUGHES was born and raised in Swansea and has also lived in Aberystwyth and London. Her stories have appeared in a number of magazines and anthologies, and have been broadcast on Radio 4. She was one of the winners of the Rhys Davies Short Story Competition in both 1995 and 1999, and was shortlisted for the Asham Award. She is currently working on her first novel.

SIÂN JAMES has written ten novels with another, *Second Chance*, due to appear in 2000. Her third novel, *A Small Country* (Collins, 1979), has recently been reissued in the Seren Classics series. Her collection of short stories, *Not Singing Exactly* (Honno, 1996), won the Arts Council of Wales Book of the Year Award. Her autobiographical vignettes of a Cardiganshire childhood in the 1930s, *The Sky Over Wales*, was published in 1998 by Honno.

CERI JORDAN was born in London in 1966, and has lived in Aberystwyth for ten years. After a career as a theatre technician, she returned to writing four years ago. Her work has appeared in magazines including *Crimewave*, *Albedo One*, *Cambrensis* and *The Third Alternative*. She has also published poetry and non-fiction, and writes a science-fiction news column for an online magazine.

SUSAN MORGAN was born in Uganda and lived in many places before moving to Cardiff ten years ago. She taught English and Drama for several years. She is currently working on a screenplay. Her first published short story, 'Fog', was published in *Power* (Honno, 1998) and is to be broadcast on Radio 4.

ANN MORUS was born in Sussex and spent ten years teaching English in Baghdad and Lisbon, and fifteen years lecturing in English Language and Linguistics at the University of East London before moving to Aberystwyth six years ago. Her short stories have appeared in *Fingerprints: Crime Shorts* (1992) and in *Cambrensis*. As Gwyneth Tyson Roberts she is the author of a linguistic analysis of the 1847 Report on education in Wales, *The Language of the Blue Books*, which was published in 1998 by the University of Wales Press.

KAITE O'REILLY is an award-winning playwright and short-story writer. She is published by The Women's Press, Minerva, Parthian and Faber & Faber.

FIONA OWEN was born in Cumberland, grew up in Arabia, and settled in Wales in 1974. She teaches the *Introduction to the Humanities* course for the Open University, creative writing for the WEA and is Director of Ucheldre Literary Society, Holyhead. Her work has been published in various magazines and journals, e.g. *Scintilla 3, New Welsh Review, Poetry Wales, Stand, Iron, Staple* and is included in the anthologies *Needs Be* (Flarestack, 1998), *Anglesey Anthology* (Gwasg Carreg Gwalch, 1999) and *Mama's Baby (Papa's Maybe)* (Parthian, 1999). She has an MA in Writing (University of Glamorgan).

BERYL ROBERTS was born in the Rhondda Valley and graduated from UCW Aberystwyth in 1962. She spent 30 years teaching English in secondary schools in England and Wales and on her retirement completed an MA in Creative Writing at the University of Bath. Her winning short story, 'A Touch Of Gloss', was broadcast on BBC Radio 4 in 1995 and other short stories have won prizes and been published since. She has just completed the first part of a novel based on her valley childhood and a comedy play for theatre.

RACHEL SAYER was born in North Wales in 1970 and graduated with an English and Drama honours degree from Liverpool University. For eight years she has worked in London as a copywriter and commercial poet, writing poetry for clients such as Rolex Watches, Harley Davidson and the Hyatt Hotel Group of Hotels. Working part time only on a commercial basis now, Rachel dedicates the rest of her time to writing short stories and anthologies of contemporary poetry in Welsh and English, inspired and dedicated to Wales. Her first full collection of poetry, *Love In Black & White*, is to be published in April 2000.

KITTY SEWELL was born in Sweden, educated in Spain (after a fashion), and then emigrated to Canada where she qualified and worked as a Notary Public. She moved to Wales in 1986 and retrained as a psychotherapist. Kitty has recently thrown in the psychotherapeutic towel to become a full-time sculptor and writer. Her first book *What Took You So Long* was published by Penguin in 1995. She writes a weekly 'Agony' column for the *South Wales Evening Post* and is on the last leg of an MA in Creative Writing. After hours, she is a CatWoman.

PENNY SIMPSON studied at Brighton Art College and Essex University. Her short stories have been published by Bloomsbury, Virago and Parthian Books. She was the recipient of a 1999 Arts Council of Wales travel bursary, enabling her to visit Berlin to research a novel.

JENNY SULLIVAN was born in Cardiff but now lives in Raglan. Having left school at 15 she returned to education in 1993 and graduated with an MA in Creative Writing from the University of Wales, Cardiff, where she is currently researching her PhD. She has written five novels for children and young adults: *The Island of Summer* was highly recommended for the Books Council of Wales Tir na n-Og Award in 1997, and *The Back End of Nowhere* was selected by the Federation of Children's Book Groups as one of the 50 best children's novels published during 1997. A sixth, shorter novel, *Gwydion and the Flying Wand* is forthcoming from Pont. And she still hasn't got an agent!

ALEXANDRA WARD is a South Walian presently living in Norfolk. Her serious education began in the late sixties when she became a student at Coleg Harlech. From there she went on to University College, Cardiff, and did research at the University of East Anglia. Her short stories have appeared in Honno's previous anthologies *Luminous and Forlorn* and *Power*, and in *The New Welsh Review*. She is a descendant of Lucy Thomas, Abercanaid, a pioneer of the Welsh coal industry.

NIA WILLIAMS was born in Cardiff in 1961 and studied History at Exeter University and European Studies at Reading. Her short stories have appeared in *Cambrensis* magazine and in the anthologies *Power* (Honno), *Tilting at Windmills* and *Mama's Baby (Papa's Maybe)* (Parthian), and have been broadcast on Radio Wales and Radio 4. She lives in Oxford, where she works as a freelance writer and editor.

ABOUT HONNO

Honno Welsh Women's Press was set up in 1986 by a group of women who felt strongly that women in Wales needed wider opportunities to see their writing in print and to become involved in the publishing process. Our aim is to publish books by, and for, the women of Wales, and our brief encompasses fiction, poetry, children's books, auto-biographical writing and reprints of classic titles in English and Welsh.

Honno is registered as a community co-operative and so far we have raised capital by selling shares at £5 a time to over 350 interested women all over the world. Any profit we make goes towards the cost of future publications. We hope that many more women will be able to help us in this way. Shareholders' liability is limited to the amount invested, and each shareholder, regardless of the number of shares held, will have her say in the company and a vote at the AGM. To buy shares or to receive further information about forthcoming publications, please write to:

Honno, 'Ailsa Craig', Heol y Cawl,
Dinas Powys, Bro Morgannwg CF64 4AH.

E-mail: gol.honno@virgin.net
Website: http./freespace.virgin.net/gol.honno/

A View across the Valley:
Short Stories by Women from Wales 1850-1950
Edited by Jane Aaron

Stories by
Allen Raine, Dorothy Edwards, Hilda Vaughan,
Brenda Chamberlain, Margiad Evans and others

This rich and diverse collection of twenty short stories provides an opportunity for the modern reader to discover a lost tradition of English-language storytelling by women from Wales, as most of the stories have never been re-published since their first appearance in print. As well as being entertaining – and often moving – in themselves, the stories demonstrate how late nineteenth and early twentieth-century women contributed to the development of Welsh culture and identity, although their contribution has since been forgotten.

The volume also includes a general introduction, and biographical and textual notes on each author and text. Jane Aaron is a Professor of English at the University of Glamorgan, and is a renowned expert on Welsh women's writing.

£7.95   ISBN 1 870206 35 5

Power
An Anthology of Short Stories by Women from Wales
Edited by Elin ap Hywel

Some women learn about power young. Take Emma –
though she's only a child, she can tell what the grown-ups
are saying through walls and locked doors.

Some women, on the other hand, keep their power hidden
inside them for years. Like Mary-Jayne Evans; though she's
dead, her body's as lovely as ever. Or Mrs Scarlatti, who's
very much alive. Or Penny, or Lily, or Meinir or Gail . . .

Honno's second collection of short stories by women from
Wales looks at where power lives – and where it lies
concealed – in women's lives. Jo Hughes, Clare Morgan,
Nia Williams and Jenny Sullivan are among the authors
who reveal that our powers are often more surprising –
and more potent – than meet the eye.

£7.95   ISBN 1 870206 26 6